Queer Kentucky is a diverse LGBTQ+ run non-profit based in Louisville, Kentucky working to bolster and enhance Queer culture and health through storytelling, education, and action. Through our storytelling approach, we give visibility and celebrate the lives of LGBTQ+ people in the great Bluegrass State. Visibility alone is life-saving. Queer Kentucky actively works with organizations and businesses on their inclusivity efforts that enhance the well-being of their employees.

Dedication
To every queer person struggling, and to all those that
have succumbed to their struggles.
Please know you aren't alone.

And to the thriving LGBTQ+ people and allies working
to enhance the lives of our community.

We see you fighting, and we're standing with you.

To our amazing readers,

Thanks to an incredible team, and a passionate audience, Queer Kentucky has grown from a small blog and Instagram account to one of Kentucky's most impactful LGBTQ+ nonprofits and an internationally known digital and print publication. Our publication uplifts Queer people in Kentucky and beyond, creating a visibility that is novel to our community. And to us, visibility is life-saving.

This past year was transformational for our organization, and we are excited to share a glimpse into what we have accomplished thanks to the confidence of supporters like yourself.
In 2023:
- We released 3 issues of our gorgeous print magazine, distributing our work throughout Kentucky and to 20+ states.
- We connected with over 300,000 individuals through our editorial content, media platforms, and impactful in-person and virtual events.
- We worked with over 70 LGBTQ+ creatives to bring you the stories, art, and events that Queer Kentucky has become known for.
- And we began solidifying the future of Queer Kentucky, hiring Northern Kentucky nonprofit leader Missy Spears as our new Executive Director, moving Founder Spencer Jenkins to Editor-in-Chief, and strengthening our fundraising efforts.

Our 2024 plans include:
- Prioritizing opportunities in rural Kentucky, as well as an expansion to NKY.
- Hiring a political correspondent to cover the Kentucky General Assembly and help make local government easier to digest.
- Diving deeper into some of the unspoken issues and experiences affecting our community, including substance use and recovery/harm reduction, mental health, housing, and the economic disparity that hits marginalized communities the hardest.
- Using our magazine and podcast to emphasize long-form interviews and stories, allowing us to hold more impactful conversations on vital issues, resources, and experiences.
- And embarking on our largest event yet, which we can't wait to announce early in 2024.

When we were younger "gaybies," we would've given anything to have a magazine like Queer Kentucky in our hands. Being able to read about queer experiences would have allowed us to find queer joy a lot sooner than in our 30s, potentially saving so many of us from life-altering and life-ending decisions.

Today, we are asking you to invest in Queer Kentucky's work in 2024 by making a monthly or one-time donation towards our End of Year Giving Campaign. To sweeten the deal, donors who contribute $240 or more (or commit to $20/month) will receive a free magazine subscription. There's a great deal of work that remains to be done, and we're committed to helping move our community forward.

It's only because of our community of partners that we can positively impact the lives of other queer individuals. We hope you'll continue to support our life-saving publication.
Thank you for all you do.

Always,

Missy (Executive Director)
& Spencer (Editor-in-Chief)
Queer Kentucky

editorial team

EDITOR-IN-CHIEF
Spencer Jenkins he/him
@SPENCERJENKSS

LOUISVILLE MAGAZINE EDITOR
Josh Moss he/him
@LOUISVILLEMAG

DESIGN
Brackish Creative
@BRACKISHCREATIVE

PHOTOGRAPHERS
Jon Cherry he/him
@JONPCHERRY

Sarah Davis she/they
@SARAHKATHERINEDAVISPHOTOGRAPHY

Clifton Mooney he/him
@GAUCHECOWBOY @GAUCHEFOTO

ILLUSTRATIONS
Andy Mendoza she/her/ella
@LAANDYMAKESART

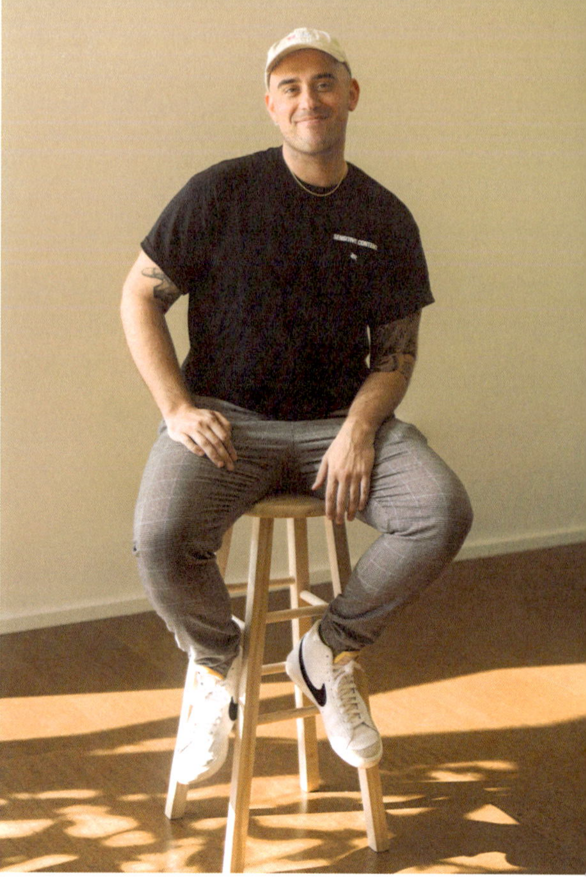

To Mary, Alli, Shaye, Kristen and Kami: I love you to the moon and back.

When I came out as gay in my junior year at Eastern High School, I was very dramatic. Not only was I aggressively leaning into teenage angst by slamming doors and arguing about the color of the sky — being what my parents called "a little shit" — but I was also figuring out that I was a big ol' homo. And my being a homo in the East End faced a lot of rejection, gossip and harassment. I remember smoking those pink Camel cigarettes and scream-crying the hit "Boston" by Augustana —

I—THINK—I—NEED—A—NEW—TOWN—TO—LEAVE—THIS—ALL—BEHIND!

— on my way home from work as a Barnes & Noble barista, thinking: "I will leave this shit town of Louisville behind!"

Coming out in 2007 was hard enough for queers. When you add in the conservative East End of Louisville, which was my home (yes, I know I'm very privileged), affirmation of self from others was hard to find. I resented Louisville. It wasn't cool enough for me, and it certainly wasn't queer enough. I needed to be elsewhere — you know, a place like Boston.

I don't think I knew of any gay teens at the time, other than the one boy at Eastern whom I would eventually sneak into my basement every time I could. My family didn't love the idea of me being gay, but they were also doing the best they could with the knowledge they had about queerness. It was an adjustment for everyone, but now, my family supports the shit out of me. Do you remember Debbie, the diner mom on Queer As Folk? Yeah, that's my mom, now. The magazine you're reading was shipped to you by my mom. Your name and address are written in her handwriting.

I will leave it at this: I was one of the luckier ones. Many of the gay boys I met as a teen are either dead from overdoses or left Louisville behind because of their coming-out trauma.

Because I couldn't run away to Boston at 17, I found home dreaming about big-city lights and an Andy Warhol-themed future with my closest fag hags and fruit flies. My friends Shaye and Alli and I would watch Factory Girl (with Sienna Miller playing Warhol muse Edie Sedgwick) on repeat, and then I'd dress them up like some Silver '60s superstar so I could photograph them. These girls allowed me to explore my queerness through art and imagination. They loved being the "Edie" to my "Andy" fantasies.

My Juicy Cotoure'd girlies would beg me to talk about the boys I crushed on while they did their best to blow smoke rings from blunts, meticulously rolled with weed from their drug-dealer boyfriends. Between inhales and blunt passes, the girls would ask things such as: "But, like, how does gay sex work? Is there, like, shit?"

We'd geek out in laughter because…well, stoned. But I also laughed because I didn't know how to answer. I hadn't had sex with a guy yet and no one had taught me how it worked.

I felt lost.

Remember, I came out in 2007 — yes, a fantastic year for the bands My Chemical Romance and Yellowcard, and the songs that fueled my gay teenage angst with lyrics like, "Give a cheer for all the broken / Listen here, because it's who we are." But 2007 wasn't that far removed from the height of the AIDS Crisis, and was only about 10 years after the murder of Matthew Shepard.

photo by Sarah Davis

"Home" became a place of fear and rejection for many queer kids in the East End during this time, and still does to this day. So I found home in those late-night blunt rotations with the best girls I could ever imagine. They were my sisters. They protected me from harm. Mary would always be the first to physically buck up to any person who dared even slightly to poke fun at my femininity. "I will fuck you up," she'd say with her head ever so slightly cocked, with a just-GIVE-me-a-reason-to-hurt-you smile. This group of young women created a cocoon of love that kept me alive.

We piddled around ear X-tacy and blasted Rilo Kiley and Sublime while riding around in one of the four Honda Civics in our group of friends. We would eat and drink at Karma Cafe in the Highlands or smoke hookah at Cafe 360, where we'd pick up a LEO Weekly to see what other cool shit we could get into. We'd put on our Vans and head to Tim Faulkner Gallery (when it was on East Market Street, and where I even had my first photo show at the age of 18) to discuss whatever was on his walls that month. We'd sneak into the Connection nightclub (RIP), braces on my pearly whites, and still be served Sex on the Beach while watching shirtless men dance in showers and cages.

And the city I was so resentful toward because it wasn't gay enough…the girls and I made it our own.

Eventually, though, I did leave Louisville several times. Once, for Bowling Green, where I received my bachelor's degree in journalism at WKU. I went on to work for several newspapers for several years. But I hated it. I didn't care to write about straight people or small-town zoning meetings. (Sorry not sorry.)

My name also became a byline for an earlyish version of Louisville.com (owned by Louisville Magazine). I was the new, self-proclaimed LGBTQ+ reporter. The seed for Queer Kentucky had been sewn, and I became dead set on creating queer content for Louisville and beyond. In 2018, Queer Kentucky was born, and it wasn't long before we were widely known as the voice for queer Kentuckians (mainly Louisville) and also for queer DEI experts. We've spent roughly six years solidifying an imprint in Louisville.

I left Louisville a second time in early 2023 for the bright lights of…Bushwick, in Brooklyn. I lasted about four months — there's something about the Bluegrass that tends to bring us all back home. The rolling hills with black fences, the big gold naked David statue in downtown Louisville — something always boomerangs us back.

And after all of the love, laughter and heartache Queer Kentucky has documented here in Louisville, it's time for a new chapter. Let's face it, y'all: Louisville is saturated with us, and there are queer people beyond Jefferson County who need their voices heard. Starting in 2024, we will begin uplifting more of those voices. Don't get it twisted, we're not ignoring Louisville. We are simply working to uplift more voices.

We've also hired Northern Kentucky nonprofit Queer, Missy Spears, as our new executive director. She will be leading the charge for our growth in the NKY area.

With that being said, and as a nod to my Louisville.com origins, Queer Kentucky has partnered with Louisville Magazine for this issue. We asked Louisvillians about their queerness and its relationship to the city, where they feel at home, who was there for them when it felt like nobody else was, the biggest issues facing Louisville's queer communities, and much more.

We would love it if you — whether you live in Louisville or not — would answer the questions too. If you'd like to, you can find the interview here: Louisville.com/Queer-Kentucky-Interview

In this issue, you will find stories of Queer Kentuckians telling tales of their beloved safe spaces, paying tribute to the loved ones who uplifted them when no one else would, laughing about their coming-out stories, and so much more.

Kentucky, and Louisville, have a lot of work left to do when it comes to embracing the queer community. But hey, it's not as bad as people think it is. Read on, you'll see.

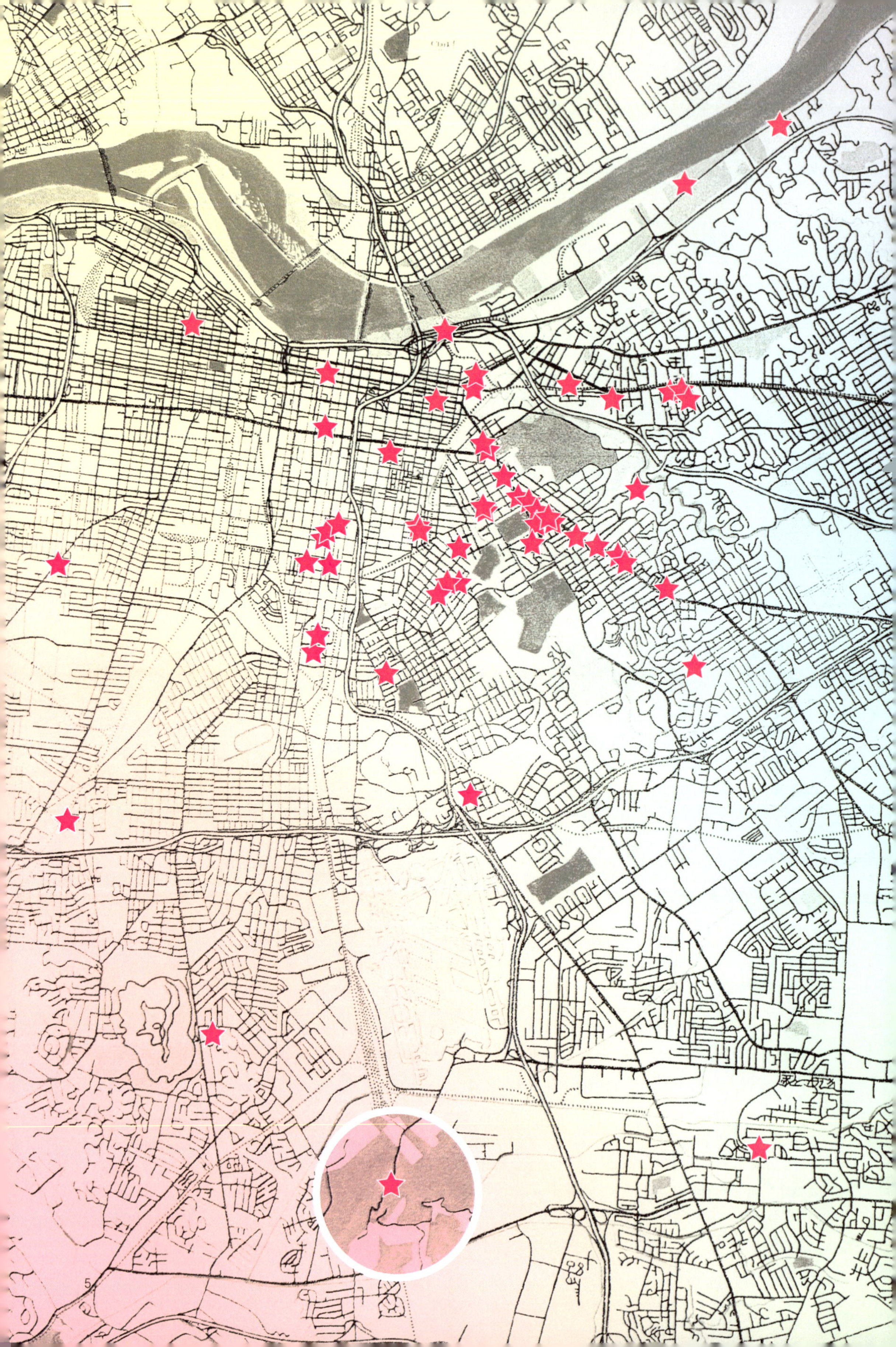

Besides your own house — or the house of family or friends — what Louisville place makes you feel at home?

21st Amendment

Aldi (Preston Highway)

Atherton High School

The Back Door

Barret Babes

Beechmont/Iroquois Park area

Big Bar

Big Four Walking Bridge

Carmichael's Bookstore

Central Park

Cherokee Park

Chill Bar

Clifton

Cox Park

Crescent Hill

Crescent Hill Library

Cry Baby General Store

Dairy Kastle

Day's Coffee

Douglass Loop Farmers' Market

Downtown Library

Dragon King's Daughter

Fat Rabbit

Germantown

Grady Goods

High Horse Bar

The Highlands

Highlands Tap Room

Iroquois Park

Jefferson Memorial Forest

Kashmir

The Kentucky Center for the Arts

Louisville Pride Foundation

Louisville Youth Group

Mag Bar

Main Library

Mellwood Art Center

Merryweather (1)

Meta

Molly Malone's

NuLu

Old Louisville (2)

Old Louisville Coffee Co-op

Park DuValle

The Pearl

Play (3)

Pop's Place

Portland

Purrfect Day Cat Cafe

Ramsi's

River Road

Safai

Sis Got Tea (4)

Shively

Speed Art Museum

Surface Noise

Trouble Bar (5)

Tyler Park

U of L's campus

Unorthodox

West Brim Salon

illustrations by Andy Mendoza

Percent of adults (18+) who are LGBTQ

3.4%

Total LGBTQ population (13+)

144,000

Percent of workforce that is LGBTQ

4%

Total LGBTQ workers

82,000

Percent of LGBTQ adults (25+) raising children

26%

source: Movement Advancement Project | https://www.lgbtmap.org/equality-maps/profile_state/KY

connection is everything

WHERE THE RIVER MEETS THE SEA. WHERE CLIENT MEETS COMPANY. WHERE BRAND MEETS HUMANITY. WHERE WE MEET YOU. WHERE YOU MEET ME.

proudly designed by

BRACKISH

a branding studio

www.brackishcreative.com

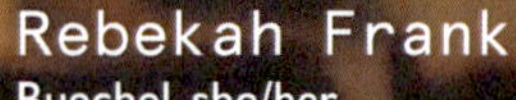

Rebekah Frank
Buechel, she/her

Besides your own house — or the house of family or friends — what Louisville place makes you feel at home?

The Old Louisville Coffee Co-op. I really love the people who work there. Community is the vibe. It's a coffee shop, a workspace, a meeting area, a teeny-tiny performance space, a hangout, a place to kill time, a place to be alone. Honestly, that's more than any home has ever offered me. I love the 'community-funding' option, I love that teachers and students get discounts, I love that there are flyers everywhere for local resources and events, I love that they keep Narcan and Plan B and condoms and dental dams in the bathrooms. People will take the time to learn your name if they cross your path often enough. It feels healthy. It feels like progress.

photos by Jon Cherry

winter 2023   10

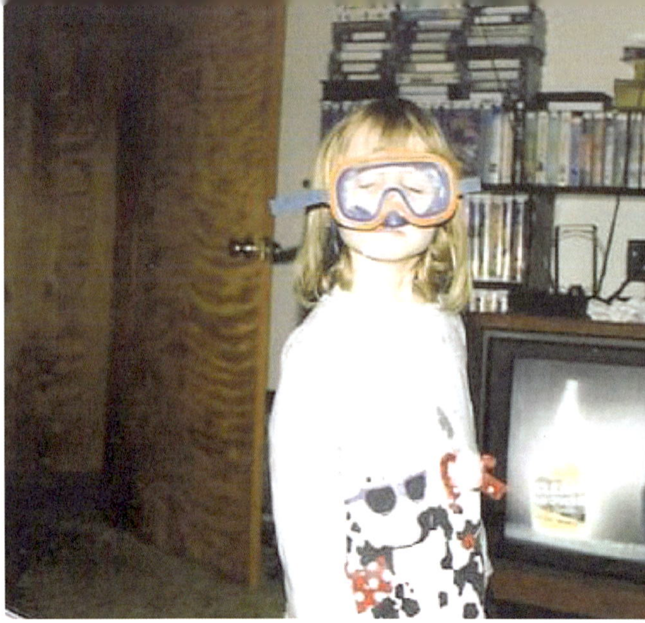

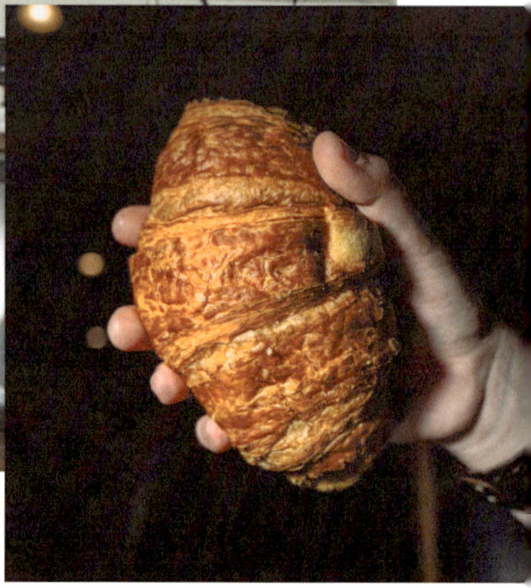

Who was the person you chose to come out to?

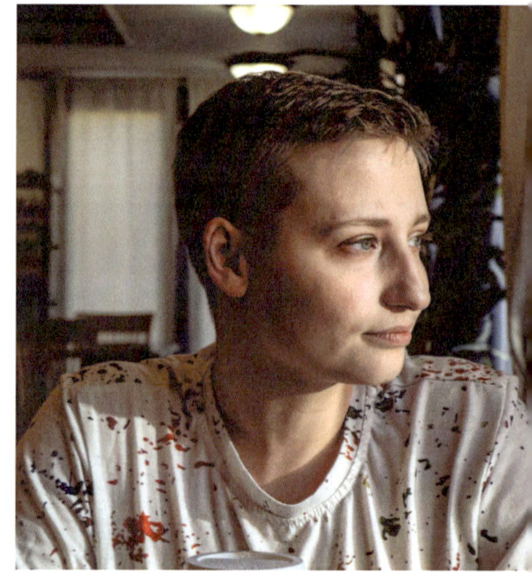

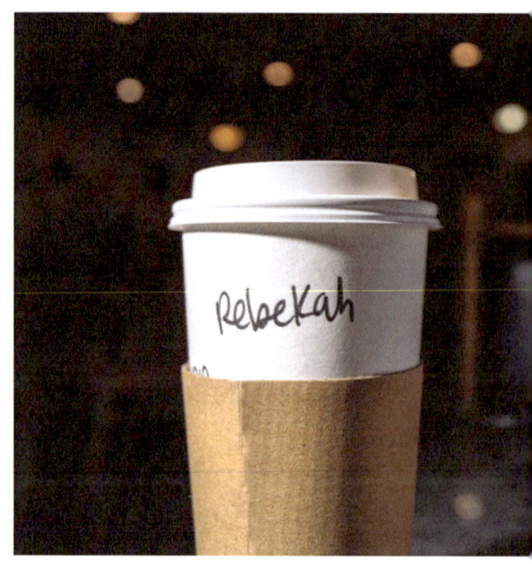

The first person I came out to was my mom. I was 12 years old. I chose to come out to her first because, even though it was terrifying, I knew she was a safe person. I think that conversation went something like, 'Mom, I'm bisexual.' And she looked at me, a little surprised, then she just looked very curious and said, 'OK. What does that mean for you, exactly?' So, I explained it in my own words, and she just smiled at me and thanked me for telling her, told me she loved me and gave me a hug. And then she probably told me some stories about people she's known in her life who were also LGBTQ+. I think she wanted to make sure I knew that she had seen the pain that being closeted causes, and that she would never intentionally make me feel that way and that I could always tell her big stuff like this. And she continues to hold that space for me almost 20 years later.

Why'd you pick that photo?

Choosing a picture that made me feel nostalgic was difficult. I've spent enough time in therapy to know that wishing things could go back to the way they were isn't an option. But this photo screams 'late '90s' to me. I was probably five or six? I know my grandmother bought that outfit for me because it matches and has dogs on it. I don't know what the swim goggles are about. There are so many VHS tapes in the background! Y2K hadn't happened yet! So many things hadn't happened yet.

Luci Lyle
Jeffersonville, she/her

Besides your own house — or the house of family or friends — what Louisville place makes you feel at home?
Pop's Place in Germantown. As a sober person, I don't have a lot of use for bars besides socializing with friends. Pop's is quiet, mostly, and divey, but dang it's the best spot for karaoke in the city. Karaoke has helped me immensely. To come out of my shell, to stretch my creative wings and to develop confidence in my gender experience by occupying a space that isn't traditionally 'queer' as authentically as I can.

Who was there for you when it felt like nobody else was?
My partner. Even before we started dating, she was a champion for me. We've known each other since before I physically transitioned, and to know that she's loved me the whole way and would do anything for me is such an incredible act of grace and love.

Who was the person you chose to come out to?
The first person I came out to was my now-ex-wife. I was terrified and had to take a shot of tequila to get through it, but I had to tell someone. And because this was the beginning of the pandemic, it had to be the person I saw every day. She was gentle and kind despite dealing with a monumental amount of hesitation at the time.

What's the biggest issue facing Louisville's LGBTQ+ communities? What do you think would help solve that issue?
Unfortunately, Louisville does not have the resources for sexually active queer folks that many larger cities have. We're in dire need of a truly queer clinic or two that can offer free resources — testing, etc. — to our LGBTQ community.

photo by Sarah Davis

Patience Fields
NuLu, she/her

I came with my wife from Minneapolis six years ago to grow our family business here in Louisville. Minneapolis is a major city with so much diversity. In Louisville at first, we both felt we were going back in time. We were wrong. The progression of the fight for normalcy in the LGBTQ community here has been astounding. Louisville has a very strong and dedicated community fighting for a better America every day, and I am proud that my wife and I have been a part of that.

My mother. She was putting on her makeup and doing her hair, usually at least a two-hour undertaking. She said, 'I love you, but I cannot condone your sin.' I came out to her because I wanted her to really see me.

More legislation to protect us from getting fired or evicted and more. Folks like [Daniel] Cameron [Kentucky's attorney general and the Republican gubernatorial candidate who lost the recent general election to incumbent Andy Beshear] want to get rid of DEI. The new laws being passed nationally and here in the South should horrify everyone.

This little girl has no idea how challenging her entire life is going to be because she was born gay. Her sister, whom she grew up with and was extraordinarily close to, will turn her back on her in adulthood because religion taught her it is OK to do so. Her brother will be distant and disconnected. If I could go back in time, I would tell that little girl that she has the strength of a thousand straight girls.

I am a lesbian. I am married to a transgender woman. People ask strange questions about this; however, I am still a lesbian. Who you are with does not define who you are.

Bearykah Shaw
Germantown, they/them

Besides your own house — or the house of family or friends — what Louisville place makes you feel at home?

The West End made me feel at home, but I've found much more community living in Germantown that I never knew before. It's calming to go outside and walk to so many places and learn about its history, while also being able to see people with your face, your skin color, interacting more. At the Merryweather, my neighborhood bar, I always feel accepted. I've only ever felt that I could simply exist in that space, and that honestly makes me so appreciative of it.

Who was there for you when it felt like nobody else was?

My fiancée, Eric, has been my rock these last six years, especially this past summer because I was at an all-time low over the loss of one of my best friends. Every day I didn't want to get up, Eric was there beside me, encouraging me and making me feel less alone. He's a man with a love that I've never known — but always feel lifted and supported. We could be quiet in a room for hours, and I'd be so happy just because he's there.

Who was the person you chose to come out to?

My grandfather Robert, when I was 11 years young. We were arguing, and I was being a brat, and I just came out and yelled, 'You wouldn't understand how things are for me 'cause I'm GAY!' And we sat and shared some crazy secrets. He's my biggest cheerleader and taught me the art of sarcasm. Always accepted me. I could've walked out in a dress, and he'd tell me whether the color was good

or not for me. After I came out, he came out to me about being 'AC/DC,' which I learned was code for being bisexual during his time growing up. He also taught me how to use a camera and see the world through my own eyes.

What piece of art — a book, a painting, a movie, a TV show, etc. — means the most to you?
A Seat at the Table, by Solange, as well as Yellow Brick Road, by Lo Village, are so raw, and I needed them during those times of finding my Blackness and exploring my emotions.

What's the biggest issue facing Louisville's LGBTQ+ communities? What do you think would help solve that issue?
I think the issue is a lack of queer spaces. We have Chill and Big Bar, but the ambiance is for white gays, older and younger. I desire a space that's preferably Black-owned for my people to thrive. As a Black queer person, it can get really exhausting always having to pull up a seat to a table not meant for me. Also, I have to mention the laws that hurt trans people trying to become their most authentic selves.

Anything about how you identify that you'd like to share?
The words non-binary weren't really mentioned when I was growing up. I was just gay, but my energy and being raised by three amazing Black women helped shape me.

David Conrad
Germantown, he/him
photo by Sarah Davis

I feel at home most anywhere, from the Frisbee field in Cherokee Park to walking around the Highlands. I also feel at home when I'm at a recovery meeting. Familiar places filled with memories. Finding acceptance, inner peace and a community.

My friend Nicole when I was in high school. She already had other gay friends and talked about going to gay clubs. It felt safe telling her, like she could keep it a secret and that she would love me no matter what.

Trans rights. Telling and broadcasting trans stories is the most effective way of solving it because more people will see a trans person as a person with their own struggles, triumphs and talents. Humanize the movement for a broader audience.

It seemed like a fun moment: picking clover flowers in the grass — at a time when I remember a lot of affection and care.

Germantown, she/they

Besides your own house – or the house of family or friends – what Louisville place makes you feel at home?
The Merryweather is homebase for my friends and me. It really became a staple after COVID vaccines became available and I felt OK venturing back out into the world. It's one of the only places I've ever felt comfortable showing up alone — knowing someone I know will be there to chat and share a drink with.

Who was the person you chose to come out to?
I don't really subscribe to the idea of coming out. I think it helps to keep people othered. Heterosexual people are never asked or expected to come out. For me, it was just more of a recognition for myself that I am interested in people in general, and that gender doesn't stop my attraction to people.

What's the biggest issue facing Louisville's LGBTQ+ communities? What do you think would help solve that issue?
Acceptance within the LGBTQ+ communities. I do think there is a real issue with racism and people feeling like they're being made to prove their queerness in order to fit in. I love Louisville, but this city as a whole has a LOT of work to do when it comes to fully accepting and honoring all of the folk that are under the LGBTQ+ umbrella.

LAS VEGAS
10
J
Q
K
A
LUCKY

ETERNITY ✿ WELLNESS

- IV HYDRATION
- VITAMIN SHOTS
- INFRARED SAUNA
- BOTOX & FILLER
- HYDRAFACIAL
- CRYOFACIAL
- & MORE!

WWW.ETERNITYWELLNESSCENTER.COM

1220 E. KENTUCKY ST LOUISVILLE, KY 40204

(502)444-8100   ⬚ @ETERNITY_WELLNESS

Custom Apparel & Branded Promotional Items

www.CustomLogoWare.com

Why'd you pick that photo?

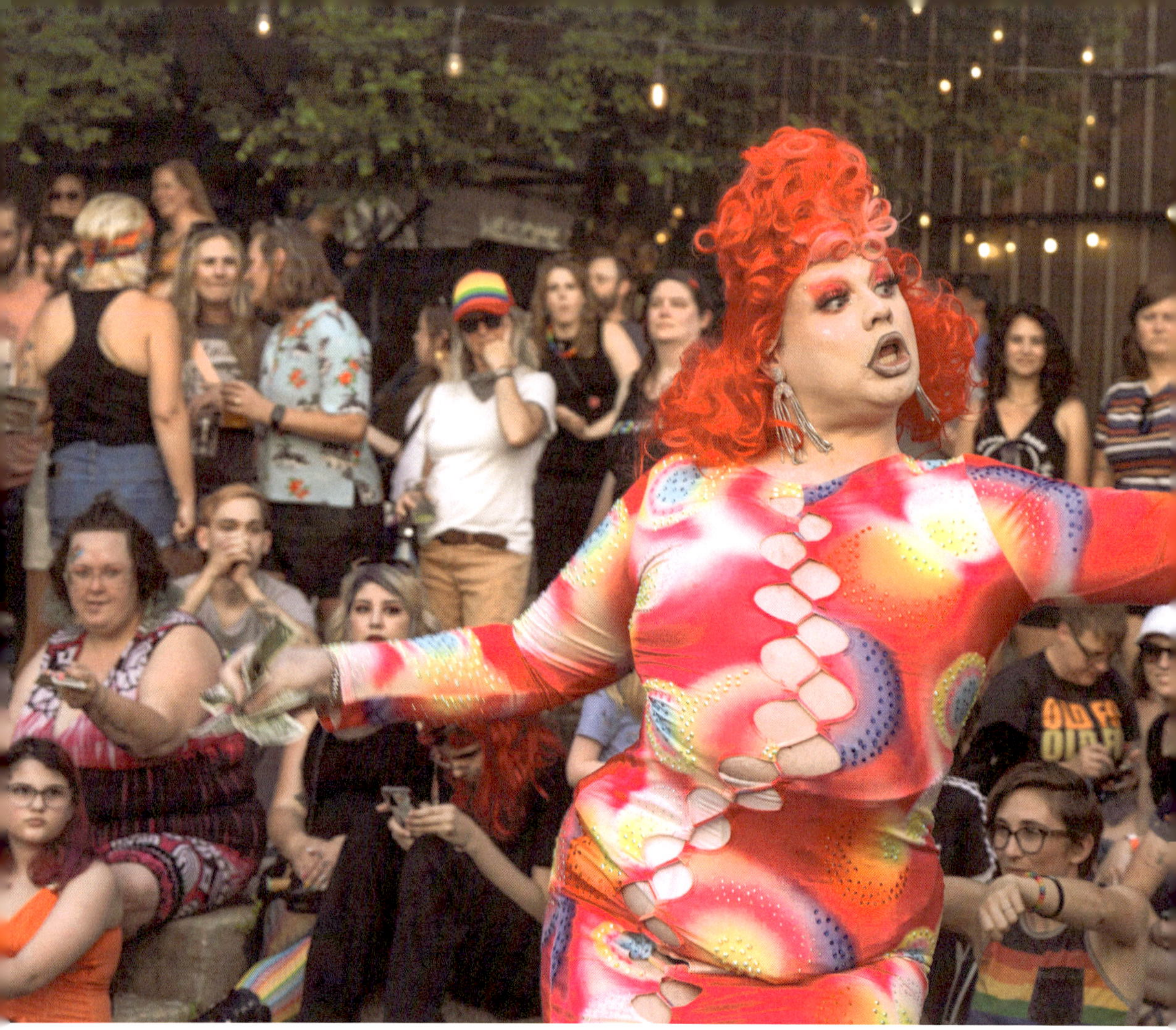

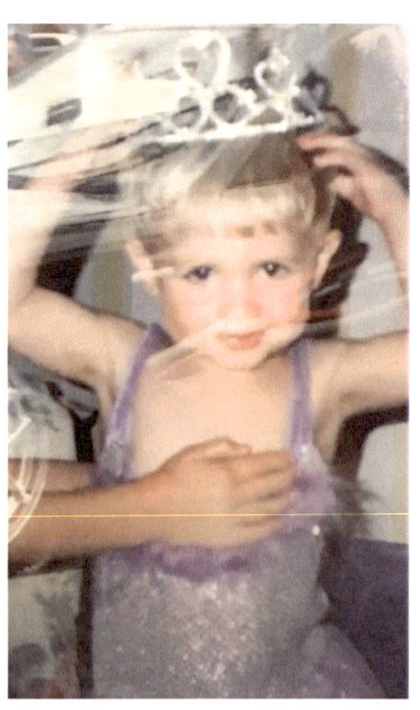

This was me as a young little boy dressing up with my sisters. Pretending to be a princess and feeling pretty. It's really cool to look back at it, knowing I've been special my whole life. Knowing no one influenced me. I was just how I wanted to exist. Dressing up is what I had fun with then, and it's what I have fun with now.

photo by Jason Morales

Tana Boots
Old Louisville, she/her/they/them

Who was there for you when it felt like nobody else was?
I still hang out with those few fellow queer friends from high school who have helped me with my queer journey. Having these people at a younger age allowed me to start expressing myself the way I wanted. One friend in particular loved seeing me dance and sing along to songs so much she mentioned I should do drag. Never really put too much thought into it before then. But her instilling that thought into my head allowed me to have the confidence to even start drag. She taught me how to do makeup and special effects. I'll never forget how much this one person helped me. She allowed me to find what makes me happy.

Who was the person you chose to come out to?
First person I came out to was my sister, who is two years older than me. We have always been close since we were babies. I watched her struggle with things, and she watched me struggle. We got each other and gained trust with each other. I couldn't imagine telling anyone else first.

What piece of art — a book, a painting, a movie, a TV show, etc. — means the most to you?
It sounds a little funny, but YouTube is what showed me queer life first. I came across a drag queen YouTube channel probably at the age of 14 and was forever changed. Seeing queer people thriving and being confident did wonders to my young mind. Still, to this day, I am a YouTube fiend when it comes to queer content.

What's the biggest issue facing Louisville's LGBTQ+ communities? What do you think would help solve that issue?
If I'm being honest, I wish there were more day events for the scene. More queer-friendly sober events. Most of the scene at the moment is mainly for the 21-or-older crowd, given that queer spaces here are bars lol. Having all-ages events for young queer minds will allow them to feel a part of the community at a much younger age.

AMI C

New York, she/her

Trigger warning:
mention of suicide.
When I was high school, I was
suicidal with minor attempts.
I would say there's a lot of
different aspects of my life that
drove me so far into depres-
sion. I am a Chinese American
woman, who's asexual, but
most distinctly was one out of
four openly atheist students at
my school. I say this because,
from seventh grade to being
a freshman in high school, the
majority of the bullying and
harassment I would get would
be because of my non-re-
ligious beliefs. The earliest
memory I have of an all-body
wave of frustration was when
our classmate AJ was leaning
up from his alphabetically
assigned seat behind Brooke,
and he was whispering, 'You're
going to die in Hell. You piece
of shit, God hates you and
everything you do.' I couldn't
take how much harassment
we took because no adult
would ever put effort into
helping us. Brooke has been
through thick and thin with
me — she was there when I
was at my lowest, back in the
mid- 2010s — and she's still
been an amazing supportive
friend that's kept me going.
Love you, babe!

I had a favorite Steak 'n Shake location in Louisville, near Meijer, that would be where most of my high school hangouts would be. My father's office in downtown Louisville was also a kind of home in my much younger part of my life. When my school would let me out, but my dad wasn't off work yet, it was where I would play around and see a sliver of what my dad's life was like outside our house. I would also say, even though you mention not the house of a friend: My best friend Brooke is a fundamental part of what I consider home. I love her to the moon and back!

Who was the person you chose to come out to?
I came out to my friends very early on in my life, as early as sixth grade. It wasn't a huge problem, mostly because either people didn't know what asexuality was or felt like being asexual means you're not straight but also not queer. So, a lot of folks never really had any different reactions due to that. When I came out the first time when there were heavy emotional stakes, that was when I came out to my dad. We were in an argument when it happened. I was invited to visit my male friend's family in California, but my father was adamant that it's impossible for a male and a woman to stay under the same roof without having sexual intercourse. And in that moment, I felt the 'fight or flight' guttural feeling of: I have to tell him. I remember instantly bawling, while stuttering, 'I'm not normal. I'm not interested in people that way.' To try to speak to my Chinese father about his youngest baby daughter and something he'll never understand. I had considered telling him for years, looked up the direct translated characters, even though I couldn't read it — all I could do was just use links and translated pages to try and open up to my father. Words that I cannot read. Everything about myself was dependent on auto-translated pages and paragraphs. We haven't talked about it since, but that day I left the house until I screamed and cried my whole life's anxieties out of me.

What piece of art — a book, a painting, a movie, a TV show, etc. — means the most to you?
One Piece and Nausicaa of the Valley of the Wind, both in manga form. In the fastest way to say this: Monkey D. Luffy, the main character, is one of my biggest inspirations but also is my one asexual-coded character that has changed my life deeply. Nausicaa, on the other hand, was an asexual-coded character that changed my perspective of the beauty and importance of various aspects of life. Both have heavily touched me and helped me in my life.

photos by Clifton Mooney

Connor Holloway

Grew up in St. Matthews, now living in Brooklyn, they/them

Besides your own house — or the house of family or friends — what Louisville place makes you feel at home?
The Kentucky Center for the Arts in many ways felt like the house I grew up in. It was a rare place that felt both intimidating and also entirely nurturing. By the age of 12, I practically spent more time there than I did in school. I learned how to express myself and be vulnerable with others. I remember it being scary, but I always felt protected by the community I shared the stage with. That type of support was essential in my personal growth and ultimately what gave me the courage to pursue my dreams.

What piece of art — a book, a painting, a movie, a TV show, etc. — means the most to you?
The Golden Girls feels incredibly nostalgic to me. A few years ago, I lost my mom to mental illness. Whenever I hear the theme song, 'Thank You for Being a Friend,' I'm immediately transported back to my parents' bedroom in River Wood, across from Locust Grove. I can so vividly recount all the seemingly late nights cuddled up watching Blanche and Dorothy make jokes I believed with all my heart I understood, but didn't. The show stops time for me and reverts me back to a place of safety with my mother. She always let me be me. I'd wear her clip-on earrings and shuffle around her white-tile bathroom in her slingbacks and sequined cocktail gowns without question. Every night, we'd read Guess How Much I Love You, and I'd mimic Little Nutbrown Hare's every move to adequately display the depth of my love for my mom — handstands and all.

What's the biggest issue facing Louisville's LGBTQ+ communities? What do you think would help solve that issue?
Black. Trans. Lives. Matter. Stop questioning it. If people took the time to really connect with people they don't understand, the impact would be lifesaving. We underestimate our own ability to empathize because we never really try. I recently began the show Jury Duty and am amazed by how much it has expanded my understanding of my own biases. It's not always by choice, but we are more segregated than we even know — our country was built that way, after all — and if we don't actively pursue diversifying our circles, we'll never be able to understand each other. And truthfully, when it all boils down, we're all the same. We just want to matter.

Anything about how you identify that you'd like to share?
I am non-binary. In many ways, it doesn't feel important to share because it's personal and simply how I see myself. I understand the world perceives me to be a man, and that's not their fault. It's the way our brains have been educated to understand each other. But I hope for more. We're capable of more. My hope, as non-binary people gain more visibility, is that people can learn not to make assumptions. To not limit your beliefs about a person based upon the way your brain perceives them to be. Whether that's a level of education, capabilities at work, contributions to a conversation, sexual orientation or anything anywhere in between — we underestimate people every day. That's something that being non-binary reminds me not to do. For that I feel grateful.

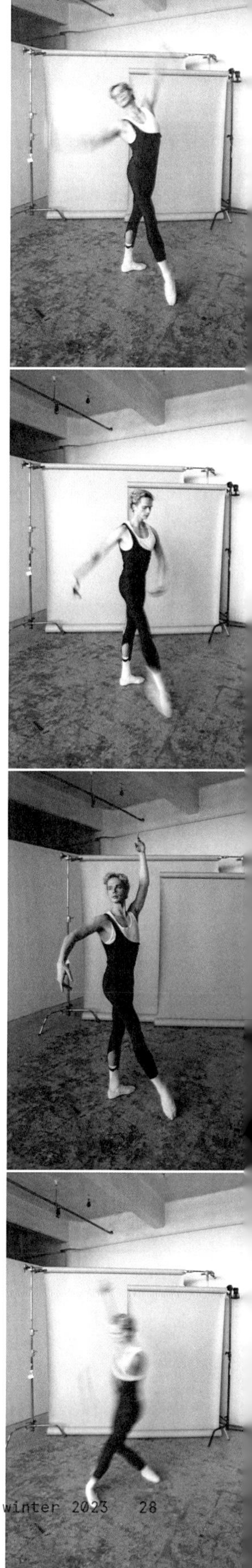

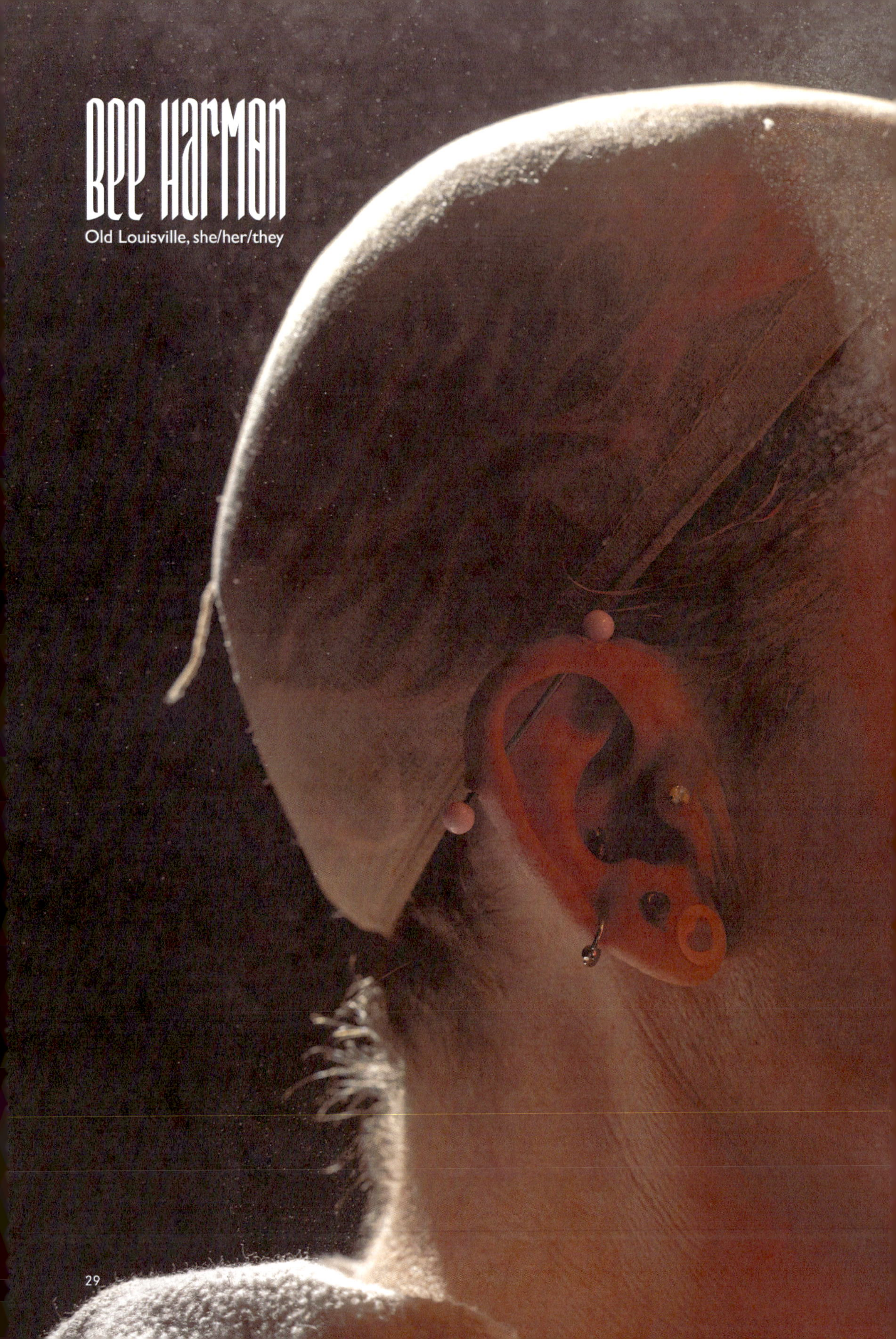

BEE HARMAN
Old Louisville, she/her/they
29

Who was there for you when it felt like nobody else was?
When I first got to Louisville, I didn't know a lot of people, especially other queer folks. I began going to the Louisville Pride Foundations to volunteer, and for support meetings, and it was there I met my friend Julian. Julian picked me up one day to go thrifting. When they pulled up, they were in leopard prints, even their four-inch platforms. Julian wanted to take me to a new thrift store, but we got lost on the way. Julian decided that they were going to get out and ask for directions. They popped out of the car and strolled down that sidewalk in those platforms — and I was in awe. I loved how they were themselves, and I wanted to emulate that confidence. At that time,

I was still in my 'egg stage,' and I wasn't wearing much feminine clothing. And in reality, I didn't know how to go about picking out 'women's' sizes, but Julian took one look at me and said, 'You look like a size 12, honey.' Such a little thing, but that day made a huge impact on my life.

photos by Jon Cherry 30

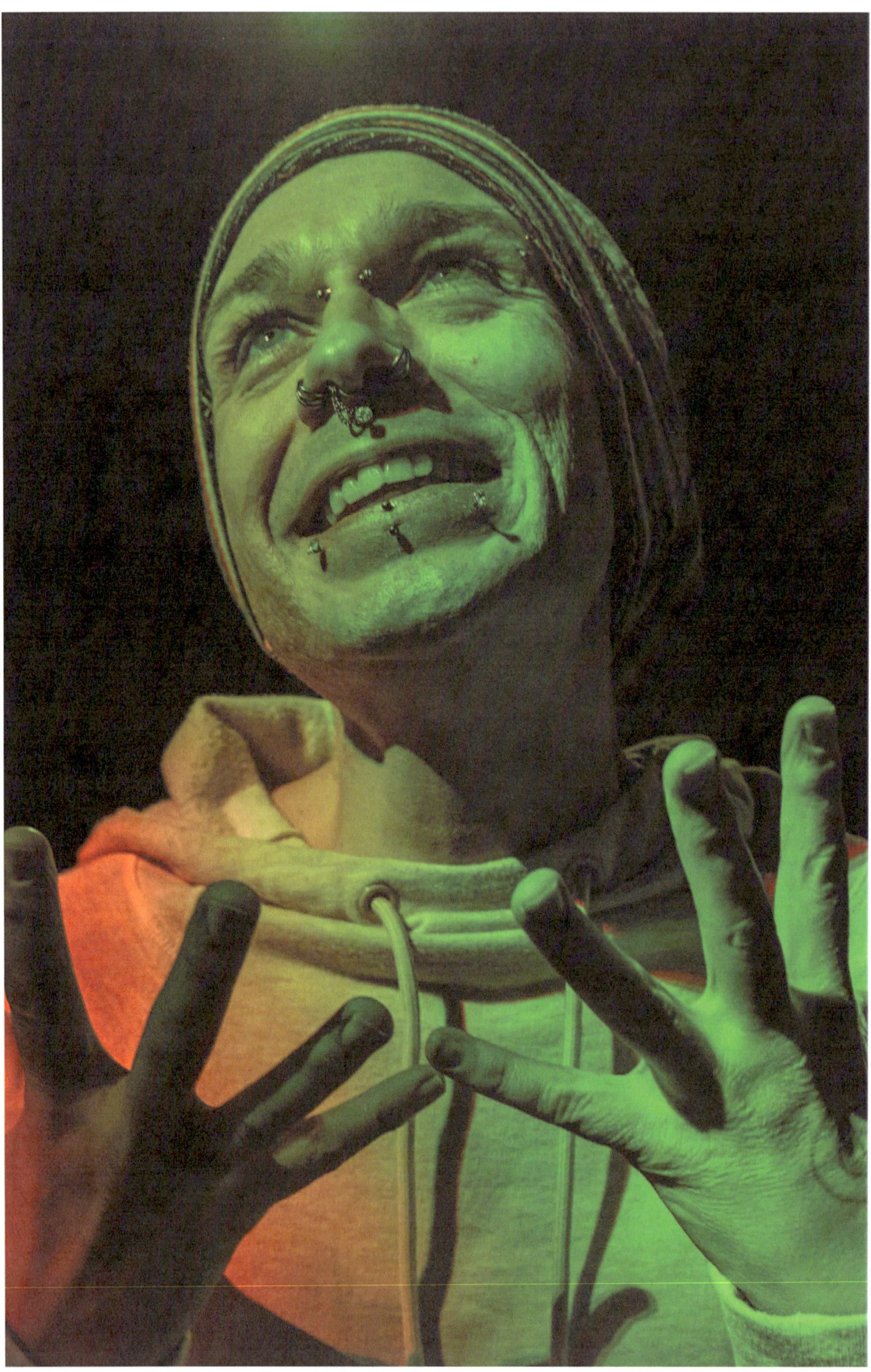

When I moved to Louisville, I had never been to a gay bar or drag club. The first time I walked into Play and saw a beautiful drag queen performing, I was in complete awe and amazement. I got goose pimples all over my body and was struck with pride. The artistry in their performance and the vibe in the theater were that of love and happiness.

From the first moment I saw my first drag show, I wanted to be a queen too. Eventually, I caught a break from a friend and got my first booking. I've done drag since August, and I love it. I get to be my authentic self, and that's celebrated and applauded. My first and most memorable drag booking was for Drag Queen Storytime Kentucky. My drag persona is basically an exemplification of my sparkly self, and I got to shine. I answered parents' and kids' questions, performed and read a book about a boy and his trans sibling. Because I'm transgender, the story of acceptance and love hit home. I'll never forget the looks on those kids' faces. The joy in the room filled my soul, and I was hooked.

The first person I came out to was my sister. She was immediately accepting, and she let me live with her and her family when I first came to Louisville. While that was amazing, I will always remember the second person I came out to: my daughter. We were always close, but I was a little nervous — not because I was worried she wouldn't accept me but because she had recently graduated high school and begun her adult life. I was afraid that, along with the stresses in her life, that my coming out would be too much to bear. One day, I picked her up and took her for coffee. As I was dropping her at her place, we sat in the car talking. I was working up the nerve and eventually let it all out. She was instantly accepting. In many ways, we have grown closer. She came up for my birthday last year and went to Louisville Pride and Play, even helping me with my makeup. Recently, I was FaceTiming her as I was putting on makeup to go out. She said she

was happy to see me happy and that I was the mother that she deserved to have growing up. We talk nearly every day. And this January, I'm gonna be a gramma! Not all my family accepts me, but knowing that my daughter and immediate family have my back means the world to me.

One of the biggest problems in the LGTBQIA+ community is the politicians targeting transgender youth and trans individuals in general. This spring, I was at several of the protests at the capitol protesting the government trying to ban drag shows and trans youth. Luckily, the drag bills failed but the bills against protecting trans youth passed. Protesting at the capitol often broke my heart. By the end of day, my voice was gone from yelling chants. I was proud to stand for my trans siblings, but it felt like I was swimming against the tide. As we made our voices known, politicians pointed at us and looked at us with disdain. I looked around and saw diversity and beauty — and wondered how these politicians could hate us.

As far as a solution, I think it will take time. Throughout history, politicians have systematically targeted people who were different. Trans youth are now their target. They claim their motivations are from God, but I think it's to stir up their base to garner support. The establishment is threatened because they are becoming the minority, and the next generation isn't becoming more conservative. My daughter and, when I was in education, most of the kids had an attitude of 'live and let live.' That's what we all want: to live our lives, and be kind to one another. Going about our daily lives, being who we are, is one of the strongest ways to resist.

I am transgender. My pronouns are she/her/ they. I'm non-binary and transfemme. I have legally changed my name, and I am registered as a transgender woman through the United States Department of Veterans Affairs and as a female with the Social Security Administration.

photo by Sarah Davis

Emmet Stevens
he/they

Besides your own house – or the house of family or friends – what Louisville place makes you feel at home?
I came to Louisville from Minnesota to solidify my relationship with my fiancé. We met online and had a long-LONG-distance relationship, and we were both sick of the miles in between. We were both madly in love right off the bat, just two opposites colliding. I hadn't lived in a big city like Louisville and thought I wouldn't grow as attached to the place as much as the person who hails from here.

Who was there for you when it felt like nobody else was?
Back when I was still closeted and in the worst fog ever, some of my favorite teachers noticed and kept me going. I couldn't explain to them everything that was going on in my life, but having an adult outside the family tell me things are gonna be OK, and that I wasn't totally messed up, helped beyond words.

Who was the person you chose to come out to?
First person I came out to was my friend Bobby, who at the time was the only queer kid I knew. Being his friend was like knowing a mythical legend, as being queer was an 'adult only' kind of label at the time, especially in our environment. I had struggled finding the words to label myself, but he saw that and swept me into a hug. I didn't have the language to say I was a trans guy, but Bobby would look at me and I would feel my whole brain and heart exposed.

What piece of art – a book, a painting, a movie, a TV show, etc. – means the most to you?
A.I. Artificial Intelligence, directed by Steven Spielberg, is a sci-fi remix of Pinocchio. It follows David, a robot boy placed into a family's home who awkwardly and earnestly navigates his new world and then is abandoned to wander the country. Pushed by his desire for familial love, he searches for the Blue Fairy. He is told constantly that his status as an android bars him from 'real' love. Do I have to belt out a several-hours-long video documentary on why that makes my queer heart ache? I first watched this movie as a kid, not fully understanding David's circumstances, wondering: Why would anyone let a normal boy be thrust into increasingly scary situations? Watching it again as an adult, I wept.

What's the biggest issue facing Louisville's LGBTQ+ communities? What do you think would help solve that issue?
A lot of us are broke, or living in crappy apartments, or working odd hours, or just trying to survive. Having a meet-up that not only fits with our schedules but also tackles the political climate is tough. We gotta meet more in multiple places, across the city, and have the reach be plausible for people who otherwise wouldn't show up.

Anything about how you identify that you'd like to share?
I don't always say I'm queer, although sometimes it's easier to say that than to get into specifics. I'm queer, but I'm a trans man who's also bi, and it took a long time to say it. I'm taking this opportunity to say: This one goes out to all the lesbians in my life who looked me right in my eyes and told me to just: 'Transition already!' I was in bad denial about my gender troubles, more so than my sexuality, and it took a couple gentle, but firm, conversations that I needed to face myself and be honest about what I was feeling. It was a long, awkward, painful, tear-filled but rewarding road. I salute you, my sisters.

Tyler Bond
Highlands, he/him

Besides your own house — or the house of family or friends — what Louisville place makes you feel at home?
I grew up in a very small town in Eastern Kentucky, and Louisville, and the Highlands specifically, is the most at home and comfortable I have ever felt in being myself without judgment.

Who was the person you chose to come out to?
My best friend, Alexis, because very early on, she made me understand from her personality and beliefs that she accepted all types of people with no judgment. Years later, she actually came out herself.

What piece of art — a book, a painting, a movie, a TV show, etc. — means the most to you?
It sounds silly to say, but truthfully: Hannah Montana. It was a very comforting show for me as a child. I remember several instances in my younger years when I was told that it was for girls, but I didn't care. I just loved it. Then Miley became vocal about LGBTQ+ rights and, eventually, out herself.

What's the biggest issue facing Louisville's LGBTQ+ communities? What do you think would help solve that issue?
Coming where I'm from, Louisville feels leap years ahead regarding LGBTQ+ acceptance. Always more room for queer spaces and events.

Why'd you pick that photo?
It reminds me of the complicated relationship I have with home. But also, I recognize and see that little gay boy, and it brings up all of the emotions.

Michael Munc Coots
Pioneer Village, he/him

Besides your own house — or the house of family or friends — what Louisville place makes you feel at home?
With all the upset from the past few years, there really isn't a place I feel at home. I've lived most of my life semi-closeted to appease my Southern Baptist family. The two places where I felt most comfortable in were the Connection and Try-angles when they were still on the scene. They both always gave me a sense of belonging when I walked through their doors.

What piece of art — a book, a painting, a movie, a TV show, etc. — means the most to you?
Rudolph the Red-Nosed Reindeer. The message that we are all misfits, yet worthy of love, rings so true to the gay experience.

Why'd you pick that photo?
My good friend Bill was always ready to support me, and we had many adventures together. He had a car when I did not, so he supplied the wheels for our outings. Bill was like a brother; we had shared so much in eight years of friendship, so it was only natural to share my, at that time, secret with him. His love and support helped me feel good about myself. Today, we don't see each other often, but when we do, our 50 years of friendship keeps us bonded.

Anything about how you identify that you'd like to share?
I am a cisgender, currently single gay man.

Alisha
Crescent Hill, she/they

Besides your own house — or the house of family or friends — what Louisville place makes you feel at home?
At Trouble Bar and Play, I don't feel like an outsider when I'm there. Retail establishments that make me feel comfortable and safe: Cry Baby General Store on South Shelby Street and Surface Noise and Grady Goods on Baxter Avenue. All slightly off-kilter — in a good way. I also feel really comfortable at the Crescent Hill Library. It's a beautiful and peaceful judgment-free zone. I really treasure it.

What's the biggest issue facing Louisville's LGBTQ+ communities? What do you think would help solve that issue?
The community seems fractured, and that prevents the power for social change that comes with unity. Many of the gathering spaces and activities revolve around drinking, which is problematic and exclusionary. There are all sorts of queer folx, but not a lot of ways for us to mingle and support one another. For instance, I find it difficult to engage in local queer culture as much as I would like because I have a young kid. I wish we could support each other more like a family than a bunch of drunk acquaintances. Also, the epidemic of homeless queer youth. It's heartbreaking that there is not a better mechanism for the elders of the community to uplift and support these kids.

Anything about how you identify that you'd like to share?
I am genderqueer and demi-ace. The ace part comes with a lot of complicated emotions, to say the least.

winter 2023 38

photo by Sarah Davis

Lar Pearl
Crescent Hill/St. Matthews, she/they

Besides your own house – or the house of family or friends – what Louisville place makes you feel at home?
NuLu, parts of the Highlands, Old Louisville, Clifton and my own neighborhoods. My street alone has at least five queer families — that we know of! — and the rest have welcoming flags. Businesses cater to the community and feel inclusive.

Who was there for you when it felt like nobody else was?
My current partner, Marcie, was there for me when COVID hit and continuing to find queer connections was suddenly on hiatus. My good friends Sarah, Lary and Tobie have always been supportive, been willing to talk out complex emotional stuff, and are some of the most open-minded and down-to-earth people I know.

Who was the person you chose to come out to?
I came out in pieces. Over different years, with different people, using different verbiage. A close friend each time was my safe space. I grew up with a very closeted yet very obviously LGBTQ dad. I've always wished we could actually connect about this, but his mental health does not allow space for that. Finding my own footing with queerness took longer and was harder than I ever imagined.

What's the biggest issue facing Louisville's LGBTQ+ communities? What do you think would help solve that issue?
Inclusion! Diversity! And I have to say it, even though it may be a hot take — misogyny. There is still so much of it floating around our own community, and it can be exhausting. Women, lesbians, feminine-presenting folks in general — who aren't in drag or trans — still seem to show up the least in representation. I'd also love to see more family-friendly community events and organizations, as queerness doesn't start in teenhood or adulthood, and often parents and siblings want to be more involved.

Anything about how you identify that you'd like to share?
I identify in what feels like a complex way. I'm feminine-presenting but non-binary. I identify the most with pansexuality, although bisexual and lesbian can feel like a good fit, based on who I'm talking to or what my feelings are that day. I always feel I'm sliding around on a spectrum, never really landing permanently in one place. My favorite word to self-identify is queer.

75 YEARS
IN THE
CITY OF
ARTISTS
CELEBRATE WITH US AT
FUNDFORTHEARTS.ORG

Who was there for you when it felt like nobody else was?
My mom and dad. They are understanding and compassionate, yet they allowed me to fail and make my own decisions and then get back up and succeed.

Who was the person you chose to come out to?
My sister. She's the person I'm closest with in this world. I trust her more than anyone else.

What's the biggest issue facing Louisville's LGBTQ+ communities? What do you think would help solve that issue?
We need more queer spaces. There are very few 'gay bars' here that allow LGBTQ+ individuals to socialize.

                    photo by Sarah Davis

I HAD TO ACCEPT ME BEFORE ANYONE ELSE COULD.

Dustin Detzer
New Albany, he/him

Besides your own house — or the house of family or friends — what Louisville place makes you feel at home?
My garage gym and Bikram Yoga Indiana. In the moments of total stillness found while giving full effort, finding the 'flow state' of consciousness, I feel truly at home.

Who was there for you when it felt like nobody else was?
My practices were there for me when no one else was: kettlebell flow, yoga, meditation. These practices are priceless and sacred.

Who was the person you chose to come out to?
The person I chose to come out to first was me. I had to accept me before anyone else could.

A place I feel completely at home is in Central Park in the summer during a Kentucky Shakespeare show. Some of my best friends and favorite actors are part of that company, and it is soul-healing and overwhelmingly joyful to get to see them do what they were put on earth to do in front of hundreds of people in the middle of a park. I have never seen a 'typical' Kentucky Shakespeare crowd; it is a mix of all ages, races, shapes and sensibilities. I've never been afraid to put my arm around my girlfriend on the bench.

That love of Shakespeare and that visceral need to have a space — not just accepting of queer theater artists, but created by and for queer theater artists — inspired Three Witches Shakespeare, the theater company I run alongside Allie Fireel and Clarity Hagan. This past May, we did our first-ever production, A Midsummer Night's Dream, in the woods at Louisville Nature Center. More than 20 people were in the cast and crew, and, in our own ways, everyone involved had been hurt — maybe by never being cast in a role aligning with their gender, maybe being misgendered by a director, or shamed for their body, their race, their hair, or just kept to the side or pushed out from this thing we love. But that process — every rehearsal, every performance — was overwhelmingly joyful and healing. At the end we all shed tears because we didn't even know a space like that could exist until we created it.

'Coming out' was such a casual, informal thing for me. I cringed at the thought of big, tearful declarations, and I knew that the people I had assembled in my community, starting in high school, would never care or shame me for my queerness.

In the same way, I also knew that my parents would never shame me either, that they would never hate or judge me for being who I am, that they are outspoken allies and champions of LGBT+ rights in a deeply red state, among their own more conservative family, and in our church. I knew all of that.

And still, I held out telling them, or even alluding too specifically to information that would allow them to draw a firm conclusion. After ten years, however, I realized that holding this truth from them wasn't allowing me to live into it fully either. Our lives are fairly distant — I live in Louisville; they live in Charleston, West Virginia — and because of that, they aren't privy to the specifics of what I do and who I do it with. But I'm also an only child, and for all the formative years of my life, they were my only reference point. I am their direct result, someone of whom they are vocally and unconditionally proud, but I was a stranger. In my mind, they still pictured me as a teenager — reserved but witty, introverted but engaged — who loved books and board games and never thought about sex or drank alcohol.

And even though I knew they wouldn't hate the person I have grown into — a bit of an attention whore, a repressed, late-blooming theater kid, an extrovert with love endlessly unspooling for every kind stranger or charming butch she meets at the bar, a steel-toed boot with a soft underbelly — I was afraid of this unapologetically queer, older person coloring the version of me they seemed to have liked so much before. And when I told them that, all of that, at the dinner table the day before Thanksgiving 2022, my sweet, soft-eyed father squeezed my hand and said, 'Of course it does. Rainbow colors.'

Tory Parker
Clifton, she/her

Kennedy Stephens
Highlands, she/her

Besides your own house — or the house of family or friends — what Louisville place makes you feel at home?
The Falls of Ohio is the place I go to often. Sometimes I don't even plan on it and end up there somehow haha. The scenery is so beautiful and being by a body of water calms me. I go there whenever I need a place to think/decompress, listen to music, or just hang out with a friend. Two other places that come to mind are Logan Street Market and Barret Babes. The vibes are always so good and welcoming.

Who was there for you when it felt like nobody else was?
It's kind of hard for me to say only one person but I'd have to say my friends and family. Everyone that I'm blessed to have in my life so far has been there for me in various ways that I'm forever grateful for. We've all watched each other grow and shed different parts of ourselves that we no longer need or want to embrace. It's been a beautiful thing and when I was at my lowest they were there. I love them so much and wouldn't be here without them.

Who was the person you chose to come out to?
I've been figuring out my queerness since I was in middle school and a lot of my friends knew without having a formal conversation about it. But I formally came out to my parents in 2020. They already knew too.

What piece of art — a book, a painting, a movie, a TV show, etc. — means the most to you?
One book that made such an impact on me was The Four Agreements by Don Miguel Ruiz. I first read it in 2020 and often come back to it when I need reminding of how to navigate the world.

What's the biggest issue facing Louisville's LGBTQ+ communities? What do you think would help solve that issue?
I love being around Black/POC queer joy. While this isn't the most pressing issue in our community, I feel not having a space for music and dance has affected me and some others. It's often a point of conversation about the lack of spaces here in Louisville. I'd love to see more spaces available where we can go enjoy ourselves, listen to music, and shake some ass without fear of it being shut down.

Why'd you pick that photo?
I love looking back at old pictures of myself and seeing how much I've changed. I feel like young me would be so proud of the person I am today.

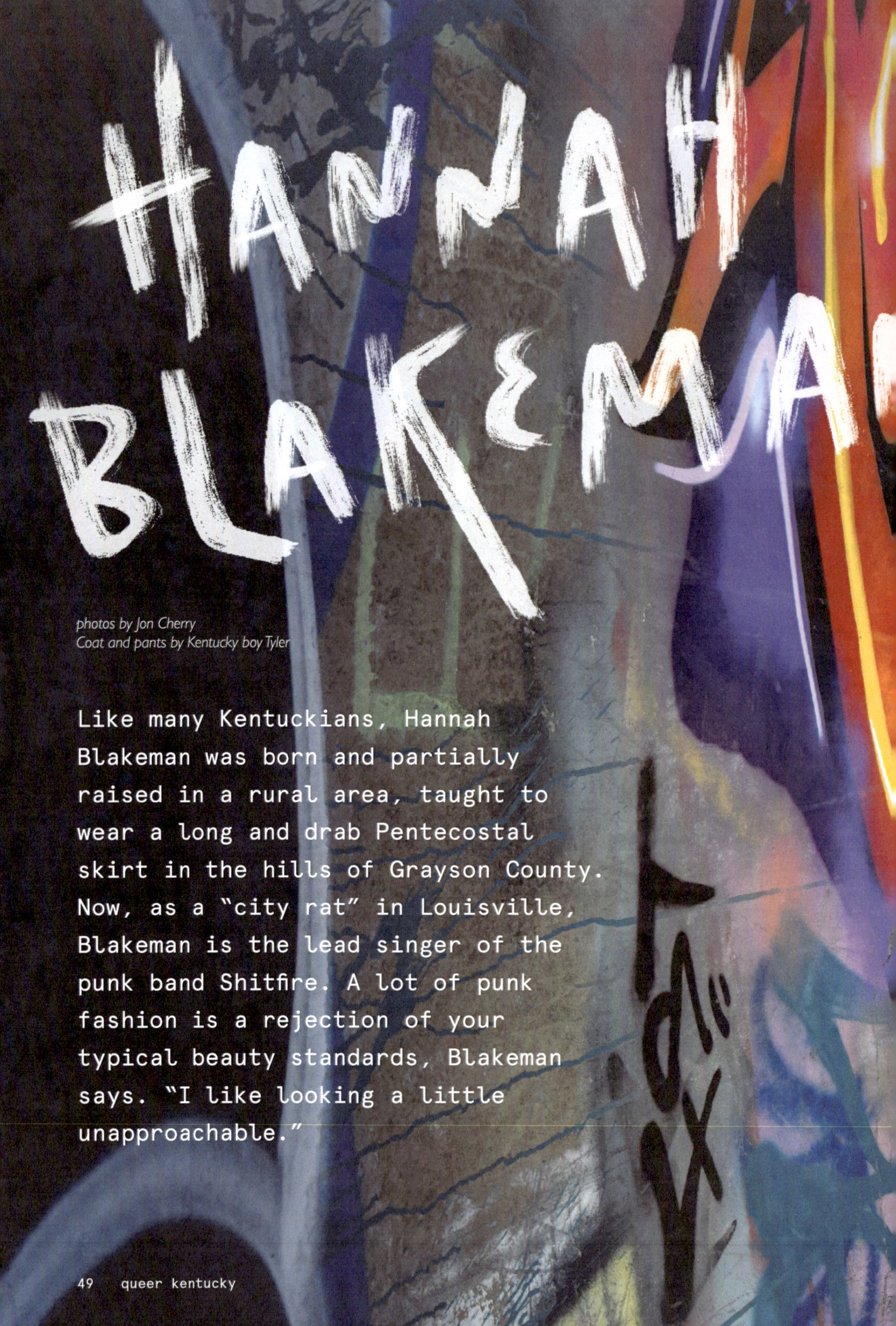

HANNAH BLAKEMAN

Like many Kentuckians, Hannah Blakeman was born and partially raised in a rural area, taught to wear a long and drab Pentecostal skirt in the hills of Grayson County. Now, as a "city rat" in Louisville, Blakeman is the lead singer of the punk band Shitfire. A lot of punk fashion is a rejection of your typical beauty standards, Blakeman says. "I like looking a little unapproachable."

winter 2023   50

Hannah Blakeman

Shively, by way of Leitchfield, Kentucky, she/they

Besides your own house — or the house of family or friends — what Louisville place makes you feel at home?

Going to shows has always felt like home to me, ever since I was about 15. Just felt like I was among my fellow weirdos. Lots of smiling and fun, lots of emotions being worked through by the performers and moshers. Everyone dresses how they want. I don't drink, so it also allows me to participate in nightlife without feeling out of place.

The Louisville skatepark — I don't see it as my home but we chose it for this photoshoot because some very legendary and very DIY punk shows took place here. I'm not a skater, so I don't want to come across as more chummy with that crowd than I am, but I've just kinda loosely been around skater punks my whole life and noticed these parallels over time. Punk shows are space for weirdos in general. Something fascinating is that every skateboarding gay or straight has been called an f-slur at some point in time, and I think a lot of the rejection that skaters and punks have experienced explains why we have so much intersection with the queer community. Rejected people bring in other rejected people to create a community and family. Skateparks have historically been safe spaces for punks and their chosen families. Similar parallels with queer

Hoodie and skirt by Kentucky boy Tyler

people. Kind of like a vogue house, but flock to a skatepark and punk life. Adults who won't judge you, but who will support your interests, take you in, give you a safe place to just be.

Straight guys into music who wear skirts and dresses have always been a thing, and the punk scene is where men can dress up and be safe. Lots of dudes in the music scene wear dresses and makeup, and it's just seen as a dope look, no questions asked.

Having shows at the skatepark makes weirdness and queerness accessible because it's always open. Well, it *should* be open 24/7. [Rolls eyes.]

Also, punk is so political. You have to decide where you stand real quick on a lot of issues.

Who was there for you when it felt like nobody else was?
Man, I don't think I've ever not had support. I can isolate myself pretty effectively, though. During my darkest moments, when it feels like I am beyond human power, I usually turn to meditation, sometimes prayer. Not sure what's out there, but I try to tap into it by talking to different types of spiritual people.

Who was the person you chose to come out to?
Probably MySpace! I learned the words bi and pansexual through MySpace and Tumblr. I changed my name to 'Blake' on MySpace for a short time, but I got accused of faking all that for clout or some shit by some straight guy friends, so I kinda just let that shut me down for a while because I didn't have a queer dating history to back me up and I felt not gay enough to even mention it.

I've never had a coming-out moment. My mom said she assumed I was queer, but we never really talked about it. I also have only entered into relationships with cis dudes, so there's probably a lot of people who don't know I'm queer. I think these sorts of scenarios are probably what lead to a lot of bi and pan erasure in the community. A lot of bi and queer women who don't have same-sex partners probably feel like they aren't 'queer enough' and don't want to take away from the experiences of more openly queer people or maybe fear rejection from the queer community. A lot of bi and pan women can end up with men because they're scared to hit on other femmes because it can be seen as creepy, and it's hard to know if you are violating that sacred trust between women.

I have followed the path of least resistance a few times just because it's scary to figure out if someone is queer when not using dating apps. I've always been attracted to women; my first crush was the older sister in Lilo & Stitch, which is silly, but I thought she was so beautiful. My first kiss was a girl when I was in middle school, and I don't think she knew she was my first since we were just at a party, and it was very casual.

I feel like there have to be many more women like me who have these desires but don't feel the need to speak them out loud since they never openly date women. It gets kept secret unintentionally. In cities like Portland and Atlanta, where it's not just straight dudes going to strip clubs, I have to assume it's easier for women to be open about their desires. Here, there are no lesbian bars anymore that I know of. I think the burlesque scene here is a great way for queer femmes to participate in nightlife. I should not have left them out. They are doing amazing work.

What piece of art — a book, a painting, a movie, a TV show, etc. — means the most to you?

My favorite movie is Terminator 2, and I've tried to imitate that vibe my whole life. I am obsessed with getting as jacked as Sarah Connor. My dad used to pull me over the fence during recess at school to go ride around town on his Harley, and I loved that chase scene where John and the Terminator outrun a semi on a motorcycle. I've always felt deeply connected to the badass characters in that movie since I was about eight or nine.

I love playing with gender in how I dress, and lately I prefer to be more masculine when I'm onstage. If I do dress sexy, I feel like

I'm in drag. I feel most like a man when I'm in a dress. It feels like a fabulous costume, and I push it to the point of camp. I like toughness in music, and that vibe is important in rock 'n' roll. I've always been adamant about having clothes I can move in. I don't want it to look like I'm there to stand still and look cute. I'm there to send a message through dance and screaming. Punk is very political and emotional. A lot of punk fashion is a rejection of your typical beauty standards. I like looking a little unapproachable.

I really like the look of being a little under-dressed, but there are still ways to make it look beautiful. Kentucky Boy Tyler stuff looks a little rural-gas-station chic. It derives from super casual — 'I don't care about clothes' — and also looks super intricate. Tyler puts such a high amount of detail in his pieces, and I love wearing his stuff. I have a piece from him that is a pair of pants made from a tiny million pieces. They look like hunting pants or gilly pants, but they're couture. I don't feel too bougie wearing his stuff to a show because it's derived from dirtball street kid fashion, and it's got soul and it's authentic. I've been most inspired by oversized looks, and I think men's fashion and streetwear are having such a moment right now. I lean into that more because being onstage and looking sexy and desirable is so vulnerable. People who get onstage with the intention of looking hot are so strong and sure-footed. I try to hide. Be a little understated.

What's the biggest issue facing Louisville's LGBTQ+ communities? What do you think would help solve that issue?
I don't know what the biggest issue is, but I sure do wish we still had a lesbian bar.

Anything about how you identify that you'd like to share?
I don't really know what words feel right. I like she/they because I feel different every day. I have used 'pan' before, but it seems to be a dated term now.

Kevin Garner
Southern Indiana, he/him

The bar the Back Door is a neighborhood melting pot that supports and acknowledges LGBTQIA people at all times. My husband and I have been going there since 2009. It's one of the few places when I walk in the door past greetings, they know what I'm going to order each time. The staff, including the owners, have always respected me and my group of friends that I take with me on occasion. I have celebrated birthdays and other special things in my life there.

My mother, who is now deceased. I felt it was important for her to know me. My mother was an educator who shared her love and support for all at a time when many of her peers and family did not openly. My mother supported my choices and me from day one. I actually came out to her after living here in Louisville for about four months. She never questioned my sexuality or my choices, which was an absolute blessing. She told me that she loved me and that I was her son, and that my happiness is all that matters. My mother applauded, accepted and supported both my holy union and marriage to my husband. He and I have been together 31 years.

Prince has been a big part of my growing up and a huge part of my musical journey. He was an artist who did not allow anyone or anything to stop him from making music. His bands were multi-racial and inclusive. He sang about current issues and gave a great deal of his time on earth to breaking down barriers associated with sex, gender, race and musical genres. Prince allowed himself to have alter egos. He by far remains an influence in the importance of inclusivity in my daily work. More important, I like the fact that, even today, you can put on a Prince song and the entire room will brighten.

Black, gay.

Acceptance. I think if we created more forums to allow people to understand how to support our communities and stop supporting roadblocks, this would be a start. I think we should create more safe spaces within our city. We as a community need to focus on the power of our sticking together and supporting each other without division. This has to come from us — all of us. Allow the various communities within Louisville the opportunity to understand the needs of all its people. I also think notifying our state officials regarding issues that affect us remains key to positive change.

SYDNI
HAMPTON

Sydni Hampton
Deer Park, she/her/they/them

Besides your own house — or the house of family or friends — what Louisville place makes you feel at home?
The Louisville Pride Foundation has offices available for public use for queer folx, and they provide events to the community, such as game nights, meet-ups and queer community events. Big Bar gives a home for queer people during evening hours and has become a home for queer nightlife gig workers — bartenders, bar staff, drag artists, etc. — and has enough going on there's usually a place for everyone to do what they want.

Who was there for you when it felt like nobody else was?
Stevie Dicks, the mother of alt drag in Louisville. Stevie is more than a community pillar. Beyond her impressive work in the drag community, she's also a fount of wisdom. She's given many pep talks to the downtrodden, including myself, and is considered by many to have saved them from themselves.

What piece of art — a book, a painting, a movie, a TV show, etc. — means the most to you?
The memoir Yours Cruelly, by Elvira, is the tale of a woman who discovered her queerness later in life but is also a story about strong will and a refusal to accept life as is. The show Buffy the Vampire Slayer is a queer staple for a reason. The queer character arcs, seasons four through seven, were a rare sapphic story on teen television. The 'chosen family' is a central part of the show's character dynamics. Queer people often find other queer people who love the show, which often leads to deep conversations about a show that finished its run 20 years ago.

What's the biggest issue facing Louisville's LGBTQ+ communities? What do you think would help solve that issue?
We lack spaces intended specifically for queer people, and too often what we do have caters to cis audiences, be they white cis gay men or cis white heterosexual people. We also lack resources for queer healthcare. Too often trans/non-binary people struggle to find dentists, or to find mental and sexual healthcare that is safe and well-versed in queer and trans literacy. We lack visibility beyond pride flags and stickers that businesses sell. Do they have gendered clothing? Is their fitting room genderless? Do the sex stores sell trans-affirming sexual-health products?

Why'd you pick that photo?
It's me and Stevie Dicks smoking a cigarette, dressed as Reba and Greta Gremlin on the patio during a QUEERDO at Play.

photos by Jon Cherry

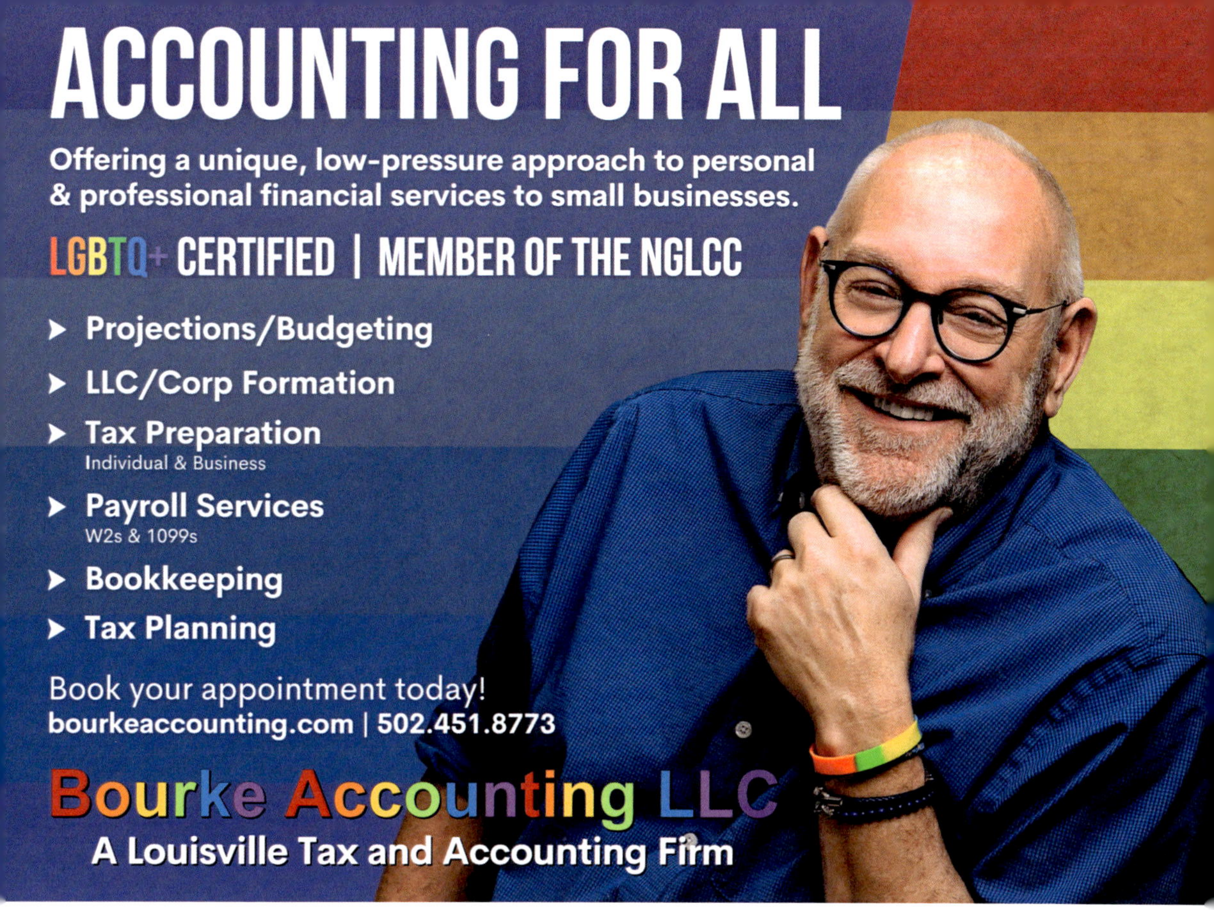
ACCOUNTING FOR ALL
Offering a unique, low-pressure approach to personal & professional financial services to small businesses.
LGBTQ+ CERTIFIED | MEMBER OF THE NGLCC
Projections/Budgeting
LLC/Corp Formation
Tax Preparation
Individual & Business
Payroll Services
W2s & 1099s
Bookkeeping
Tax Planning
Book your appointment today!
bourkeaccounting.com | 502.451.8773
Bourke Accounting LLC
A Louisville Tax and Accounting Firm

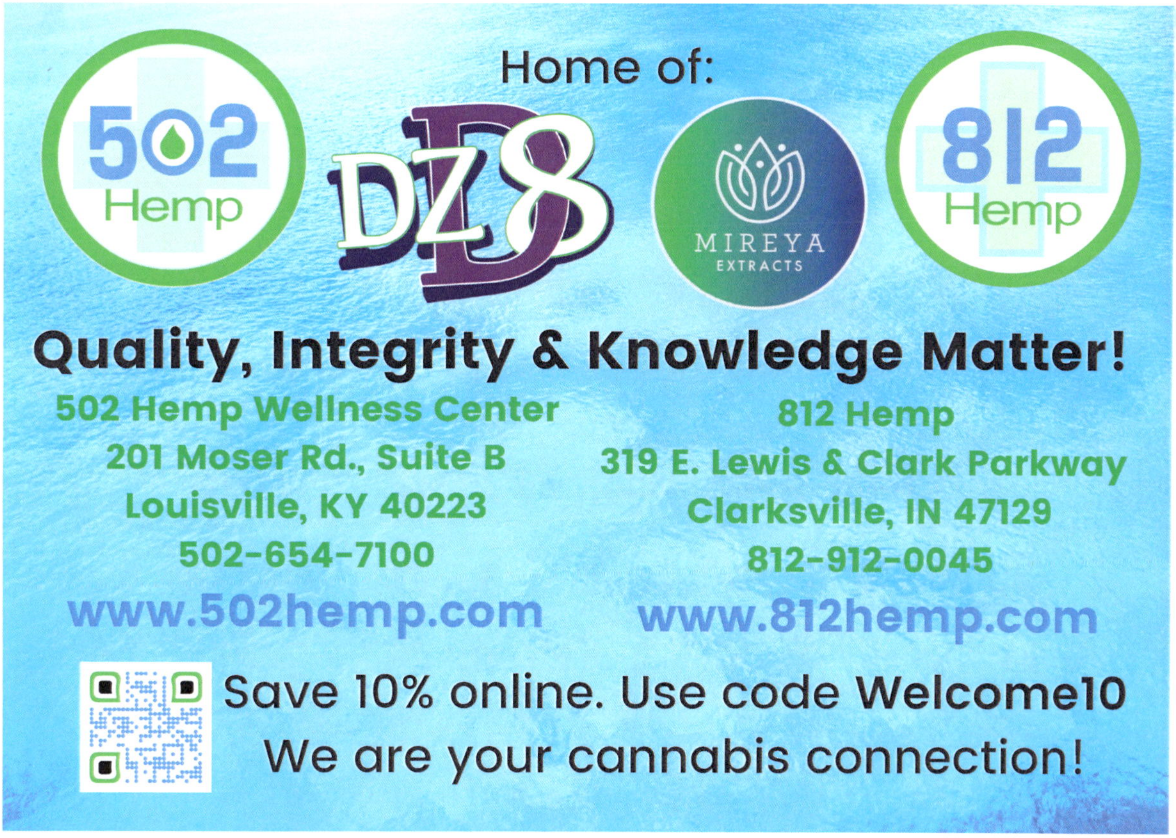
502 Hemp
Home of:
DZ8
MIREYA EXTRACTS
812 Hemp
Quality, Integrity & Knowledge Matter!
502 Hemp Wellness Center
201 Moser Rd., Suite B
Louisville, KY 40223
502-654-7100
www.502hemp.com
812 Hemp
319 E. Lewis & Clark Parkway
Clarksville, IN 47129
812-912-0045
www.812hemp.com
Save 10% online. Use code Welcome10
We are your cannabis connection!

Belle Townsend

St. Joseph, she/they, Queer Kentucky Political Correspondent

Besides your own house — or the house of family or friends — what Louisville place makes you feel at home?
Cherokee Park, Tyler Park and other local parks make me feel at home. To be sitting with the trees and knowing that the city has maintained these areas is special to me. I feel similarly when at any of Louisville's libraries.

Who was there for you when it felt like nobody else was?
My girls. I was socialized as a girl to be a woman, and I am still figuring out how girlhood fits into my overall identity. What I do know is that, since I was a child, I have had a friend who was a girl who was also a listener. I had a friend who was a girl who was gentle, who was fierce, who was unapologetic, who was passionate, who was everything I needed at the time. Life is a series of cycles, of loss and of growth. In every cycle, from the time that I was in pre-school to now at 23, I have been carried by the girls around me. When I traversed rural Kentucky as a young queer girl, I did not know who I was. But it seemed people around me knew who I was to the extent that they isolated me. When I wore my hair in a slicked-back ponytail and wore sneakers, the mean girls at my Christian school called me a lesbo. Meredith played ball with me at recess that day. When I didn't get invited to the movies because I was different, Sarah and I made popcorn and watched Netflix at home. When I didn't know how to exist in a growing and ever-feminizing body, Riley defended me when the girls in the locker room asked why I wore two sports bras instead of one pushup bra. When I came out to my mother and felt rejection unlike anything I had ever known, Tabitha took me thrifting and reminded me that my world would be bigger than it was then. When I was the young, outspoken, tattooed, radical voice in the room, Carmellia's face lit up when I walked in. She told me she was so glad I was there. I have been blessed to keep some of these people in my life, but some of them have gone their own ways. And while that can be a devastating thing to think about, it can also be a beautiful thing — to carry someone in the moment they need it most. In navigating my life, in navigating queerness, it was always girls who were there for me when nobody else was. There is something to say about how we carry each other, always, even if we are different and we don't understand everything about each other.

Who was the person you chose to come out to?
I knew that I was different, and any time anyone spoke about queerness, I felt like all eyes were on me. I grew up Southern Baptist in rural Western Kentucky, and I do not remember the first time I really came out to someone. I explored queerness after moving to Boston for school, although I had already reckoned at that time that I was in the queer community. I did make a Facebook post after I had my first serious girlfriend. I shared this with my community, which does include a lot of people from my home, and I was taken aback at how people responded. Comment after comment and message after message about how folks supported me and were so thankful for my willingness to share my identity. This included immediate family members I was nervous to speak to in person, fearing they might literally hurt me. It taught me how people can always surprise us, and most of all, it taught me that love of community and people often transcend the divisive bullshit spewed upon us to separate us.

Anything about how you identify that you'd like to share?
I am queer in both my sexuality and my gender identity. I consider myself to be both non-binary and trans, attempting to live every day beyond the binaries.

Levi House
Just moved to Lexington from Shelby Park, he/him

Who was there for you when it felt like nobody else was?
My sister has always been there for me when I have felt totally alone. Sometimes it has felt like she knows me better than I do.

Who was the person you chose to come out to?
I chose to come out as trans to my first girlfriend because I knew she was kind. I didn't know what she would say or if she would be cool with it or continue to date me, but I knew that I couldn't keep it to myself anymore, and I trusted her. She was one of the first people who made me feel like just 'me' when I was around them, instead of just 'a girl.' I knew she could keep a secret until I wanted it to not be one.

What piece of art — a book, a painting, a movie, a TV show, etc. — means the most to you?
Glamorous, the Netflix series, depicts a trans character in a way that makes their being trans the least interesting thing about them. The character's life is so full, and we learn so much about them before being let in on the fact that they're trans. We also see how their own understanding of, and relationship to, their gender develops as normal aspects of their life continue and feed into this discovery. We're also shown how important real community is for queer and trans people while being reminded to be fierce, to stay true to ourselves, and that doing so is hard work and takes bravery and guts, and that we are worth it and deserving of living our truth

photos by Jon Cherry

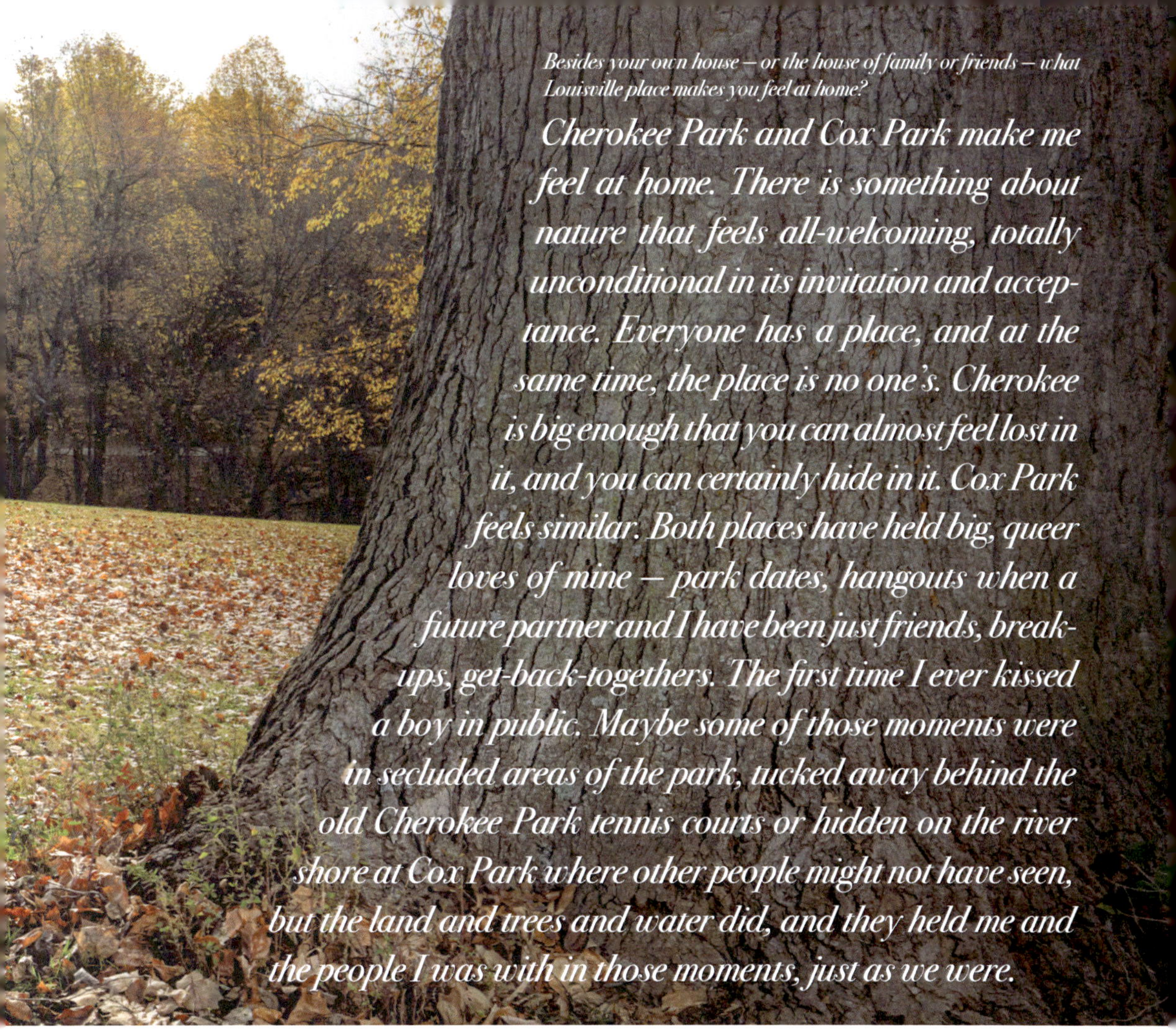

Besides your own house – or the house of family or friends – what Louisville place makes you feel at home?

Cherokee Park and Cox Park make me feel at home. There is something about nature that feels all-welcoming, totally unconditional in its invitation and acceptance. Everyone has a place, and at the same time, the place is no one's. Cherokee is big enough that you can almost feel lost in it, and you can certainly hide in it. Cox Park feels similar. Both places have held big, queer loves of mine – park dates, hangouts when a future partner and I have been just friends, breakups, get-back-togethers. The first time I ever kissed a boy in public. Maybe some of those moments were in secluded areas of the park, tucked away behind the old Cherokee Park tennis courts or hidden on the river shore at Cox Park where other people might not have seen, but the land and trees and water did, and they held me and the people I was with in those moments, just as we were.

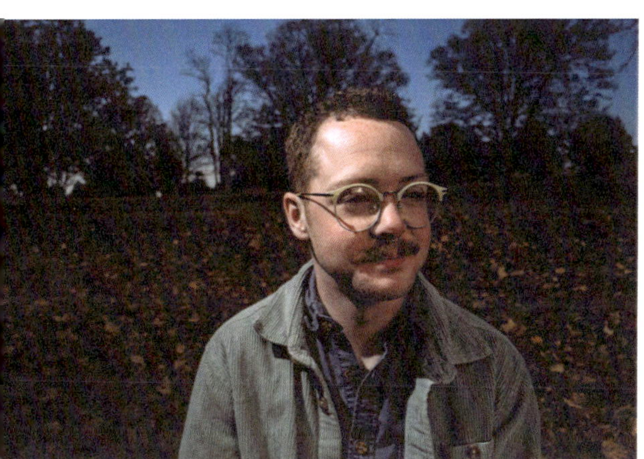

and allowing ourselves to discover what our truth fully is. It felt so beautiful and important to see a trans character portrayed as essentially a normal person, who is layered and complex and figuring it out and living a full and beautiful life. Note: Using gender-neutral pronouns to potentially avoid spoilers.

There is a book called American Boys that captures stories and portraits of trans masc people across the U.S., all of them very different, but all of them standing so proud. Looking through it and seeing so many people who are so full of life and pride makes me feel powerful, brave and proud. It makes me feel less alone. It makes me feel like one of a kind. It makes me feel like there is so much opportunity to learn and to share with one another and that there are so many people like me out there. It also feels empowering and encouraging to know that there are people who are documenting the experiences of trans people, especially in a time when more and more efforts appear to erase them.

Josiah
Old Louisville, he/him

Who was there for you when it felt like nobody else was?
My friend Stephanie. I began working with her almost ten years ago, and eventually we became friends. She took me under her wing in many ways. I see her as sort of my queer mom. I think we bonded over shared mental and physical illnesses and also over being nerdy and weird. She is surly and bisexual and darkly funny and has a binder of Stardew Valley information. When everyone else had somehow abandoned or betrayed me, she was there still to reach out to. She's been a constant supporter from my teenage years into adulthood, and I can't picture what my life would look like without her in it.

Who was the person you chose to come out to?
I first came out to a Christian youth counselor, and when I did, I couldn't say the words myself. I simply told him I had something to tell him. I sat in silence for a long time, and he eventually began listing all the things young people had told him, from their engaging in self-harm to perverted things like molesting their siblings. Eventually he said 'gay,' and I nodded at that one. He was the first person I had trusted, and it was largely because he seemed to be my friend and hung out with me despite my 'oddities' — what I now know to be autistic traits.

What piece of art – a book, a painting, a movie, a TV show, etc. – means the most to you?
Steven Universe. Over the course of the show, it becomes an analogy for healing from family trauma, queer identity. It is also just very pretty to look at.

Anything about how you identify that you'd like to share?
I've been exploring the nuances of terming myself agender vs. non-binary, and how the two are different and how they might overlap.

photos by Sarah Davis

John E
Middletown, he/him

Besides your own house — or the house of family or friends — what Louisville place makes you feel at home?
Play is where my now-husband and I got to know each other. It's the place we'd go to when we wanted to celebrate life's events, or mourn with the community like after Pulse nightclub, or be in a place where we didn't have to worry about being ourselves.

What's the biggest issue facing Louisville's LGBTQ+ communities? What do you think would help solve that issue?
General acceptance of the entire LGBTQ community and, specifically, the trans community. Visibility matters, and having a unified voice where we support each other is key to improvements.

photo by Sarah Davis

Victoria Syimone Taylor
Highlands, she/they

Who was there for you when it felt like nobody else was?
Amirage Sailing. I trusted her with my deepest
shame and secrets. She and I had a long road
to sisterhood, but she listened and loved me
and was forgiving, loyal and honest. I believe
she was an angel on this earth.

Who was the person you chose to come out to?
I never had to come out; my flame burned
very, very bright lol. My most supportive family member is my Aunt Jo, who has always been
my cheerleader and champion and has been
there when I needed love, care and support.

*What piece of art — a book, a painting, a movie, a TV
show, etc. — means the most to you?*
To Wong Foo, Thanks For Everything! Julie
Newmar is a movie I love and have seen
hundreds of times. I just understand the hard
work and dedication it took to create this
amazing piece of art. It made me feel seen and
loved through the laughter and coded slang
used in the movie.

*What's the biggest issue facing Louisville's LGBTQ+
communities? What do you think would help solve that
issue?*
Communication between cultures. We don't
have the skills or language to facilitate proper
sit downs to discuss how similar we are, and
what we could do to bridge this culture gap.

Calvin Silver
UofL campus/Old Louisville, he/him

Besides your own house – or the house of family or friends – what Louisville place makes you feel at home?
The Big Four Walking Bridge makes me feel most at home. It is a place that my boyfriend and I often visit together on dates because it is beautiful and also free. I will admit that what makes me feel at home is not the bridge itself or the other people there, but instead the company I am with. Louisville has never felt all that friendly to me and doesn't really feel like my home, so I find home in other people rather than in places.

Who was there for you when it felt like nobody else was?
My boyfriend, Parker, has been there through it all. I don't want to say that he was there 'when no one else was,' because I am lucky to have a strong support system. But when I didn't want anyone else there, he was the person who I always wanted by my side. He's seen my best and worst and everything in between and sticks by me regardless. I love him so goddamn much.

Who was the person you chose to come out to?
When I did my whole 'coming out to the world' production — because it certainly felt like a production! — I first came out to my RA the summer I was away at the Governor's Scholars Program. I did my Governor's Scholar summer at Bellarmine, so I suppose Louisville was the place I first really came into my own. I told my RA because she had been openly and unabashedly accepting of queer people and had talked about her advocacy for queer youth that had stemmed from her thesis paper.

What piece of art — a book, a painting, a movie, a TV show, etc. — means the most to you?
The movie Ponyo is one of my boyfriend's and my favorite movies of all time. It is so sweet and cute and shows a really innocent form of love. I also have a particular fondness for the Kentucky writer Silas House, whom I've met a few times and whose books have been an influential presence in my life since I was in early high school. I love the emotion in his writing, the refusal to shy away from hard things.

What's the biggest issue facing Louisville's LGBTQ+ communities? What do you think would help solve that issue?
Hatred and bigotry. The people committing homophobic and transphobic acts aren't flukes or monsters — they are normal, everyday people. They are the people you pass at the grocery store and at school. They are the people who work at the DMV and in school administration. That is what scares me the most. Fearmongering works for a reason, particularly when targeting already vulnerable groups. Public opinion helps to shape our access to public accommodations, bathrooms, healthcare, personal identification and just day-to-day life. I don't know how to solve it because I cannot convince someone who hates me on a fundamental level that I'm not what they think I am.

Anything about how you identify that you'd like to share?
I am a trans gay guy. I've been out for four years and on T for nearly as long. Those are the most important bits for now.

Hmmm, I don't think I ever
officially came out to anyone.
Just kind of started mentioning
going on dates with not-men.

Megan Miller
Highlands Douglass, she/her

Besides your own house — or the house of family or friends — what Louisville place makes you feel at home?

I'm originally from Michigan, but I've been in the Louisville area for ten-ish years. I feel at home walking in my neighborhood, at Big Rock Park and at the Douglass Loop Farmers' Market. As much as I love to drive to Jefferson Memorial Forest or even Red River Gorge to go for a hike, sometimes I don't have the time or energy. Walking in my neighborhood resets me and grounds me.

Who was there for you when it felt like nobody else was?

Margret, a friend I reconnected with earlier this year. The relationship we have developed has grown into such a caring friendship. I feel like we have been there for each other through hard and difficult times this year.

What's the biggest issue facing Louisville's LGBTQ+ communities? What do you think would help solve that issue?

For me, it has been trying to find spaces that are not alcohol-centered. I am happy to be participating in a new bicycling group, Queers with Gears 502.

Teresa Willis
Highlands, she/her

Why'd you pick that photo?
This is me and my mom, my sister posing us in front of the tree by the garage back when photography was a precious process. I'm about 12, so my mom would've been 52. This photo encapsulates so much. A warm fall day in Valley Station. The geekiest version of myself on full display. Our easy relationship before the turbulence of adolescence really set in.

What's the biggest issue facing Louisville's LGBTQ+ communities? What do you think would help solve that issue?
Nothing is more invisible to society than a childless, husbandless, post-menopausal woman, no matter how they identify. If they are un-partnered and queer, it can be very lonely. The bar scene isn't appealing. There are welcoming churches now, but it's hard to shake the old pain of alienation. We end up depending on each other. But I know there are others out there who are falling through the cracks. Women's earning power was pretty limited in the boomer and X generations, and we didn't have the benefit of a male partner's salary throughout our lives like many of our straight counterparts. Louisville Pride Foundation is a great start for our community in general, but we need a concerted look at our aging population and need LGBTQ+-focused support of all kinds — navigating systems, financial advice, estate planning, aging-in-place strategies, community events, mental-health services. Some entity that sees us in the context of our sensitivities and traumas, as well as our talents, wisdom and the legacy we represent — and gives us a framework for resources.

Anything about how you identify that you'd like to share?
I'm bisexual, but I like 'queer' as an identifier. It unites us as non-heteronormative, which is a specific experience, no matter the era.

SUPPORT QUEER JOURNALISM

www.queerkentucky.com

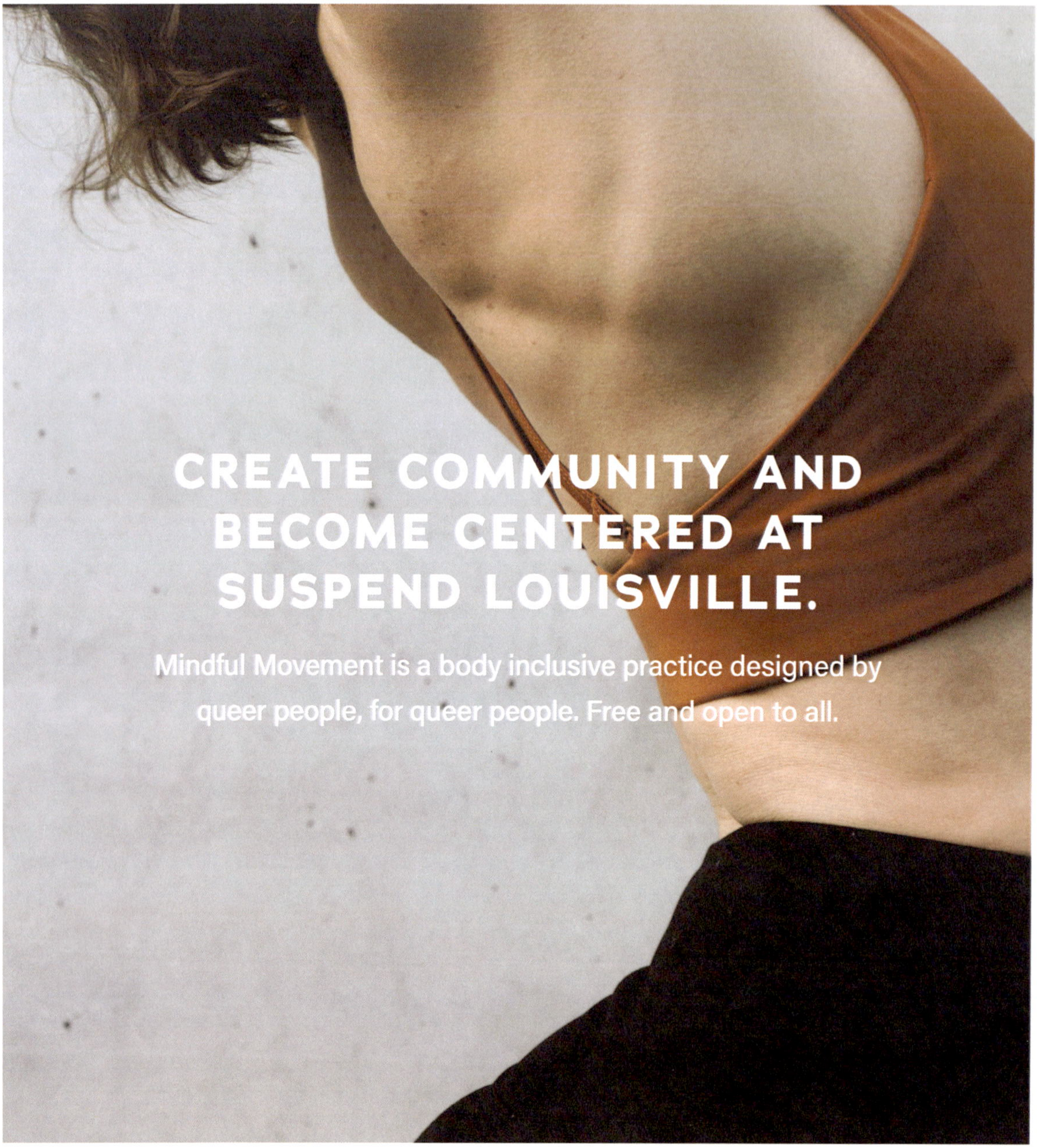

CREATE COMMUNITY AND BECOME CENTERED AT SUSPEND LOUISVILLE.

Mindful Movement is a body inclusive practice designed by queer people, for queer people. Free and open to all.

Sundays 10 - 10:50 a.m.

721 E Washington St, Louisville, KY 40202